About the Author

Nicolas Youssef is a first-time author who was raised in the Syriac Orthodox community of Turkish origin. Born in Lebanon, Nicolas spent most of his childhood in Beirut, where he attended a Catholic school. As he grew up in the midst of the civil war, he questioned why there was so much injustice in the world, and he wondered what he could do to make a positive difference. With *Secrets of the Angels*, Nicolas hopes that his readers will understand life's moral dilemmas and learn how to attain true happiness and salvation. Currently, Nicolas resides in Sweden.

Secrets of the Angels

Nicolas Youssef

Secrets of the Angels

Olympia Publishers
London

www.olympiapublishers.com
OLYMPIA PAPERBACK EDITION

A CIP catalogue record for this title is
available from the British Library.

ISBN: 978-1-83543-528-1

This is a work of fiction.
Names, characters, places and incidents originate from the writer's
imagination. Any resemblance to actual persons, living or dead, is
purely coincidental.

First Published in 2025

Olympia Publishers
Tallis House
2 Tallis Street
London
EC4Y 0AB

Printed in Great Britain

Dedication

To the Mother who watches over us and does not bat an eyelid.
From her heart flows endless love and tenderness. I raise this
book to her.

Foreword

I truly enjoyed reading the book entitled *Secrets of the Angels,* written by the writer and thinker Nicolas Youssef. It is a very useful book, which the author wrote in a smooth style. Nicolas Youssef adopted an elaborate fragmentation technique that refers to the beginnings of wisdom and philosophy (i.e., the philosophy of religion). In the book's chapters, there is an accurate analysis of the emotional status and the pain experienced by Tom, the main character in the story.

Tom plays a pivotal role in the narrative construction of the short novel as well as in the search for truth by asking existential questions. I also noticed that the text is based on 'intertextuality.' It is a fictional, philosophical-religious, and poetic text all at the same time.

After reading the short novel, I invite readers to closely see the author's explanation of two theories that he related to it: the theory of fallen angels and a modern theory of the Holy Trinity mystery.

Dr. Marwen Alkilani
Writer and translator

For Definition

In the book, I will use two important terms. The first is 'hypostasis,' which means 'an entity that shares nature and essence with another entity and is united with it in one being or one body, regardless of whether it is spiritual or material. Each of these two or more hypostases has a free will and a characteristic that differs it from the other.'

The second term is 'inner consciousness,' which, according to my view and belief, has an entity and free will, whether it is within God or within man. Within this entity, there is a law of high morals and noble feelings. Whenever I mention the term 'inner consciousness' in the book, remember that I mean it in this sense.

California 1984

Chapter One

Every day, the dawn broke behind the eternal Sierra mountains, and the sun rose from its den to gradually spread its warm, golden rays onto nature. In those magical moments, the cool breeze caressed the damp tips of grass and flowers, and birds started to sing from above the branches to inspire creatures to start their day.

In that beautiful and calm atmosphere, Tom woke up every day at dawn, had his breakfast, and went out to the garden of the house to allow his senses and soul to enjoy the charms of those stunning moments until the sun embraced the city of Burbank with love and tenderness.

Every morning in the city was similar to each other, except on Sundays when the faithful went to church to worship and glorify the Lord, the Creator of the heavens and the earth. The Aphram family had always fulfilled this religious duty. Since Mr. and Mrs. Aphram arrived in the state, they had fulfilled their religious duties, and they continued to raise their children in piety, love of God, and adherence to His commandments.

At 9:50 a.m., the Aphram family was ready, waiting for the son, Tom, to prepare to go with them. Everyone got in the car and headed toward the church. On the road, the father said to his son, "Your brother Marcus' wedding to Natalie is in two weeks, and God willing, we will also be happy with your wedding one day."

Tom replied with joy that immersed him, "May the Lord bless this good intention; Marcus has been waiting so long for this dream to come true. As for me, I will wait my turn to achieve my dream as well."

Tom was twenty-three years old, and Markus was twenty-five years old. They also had a brother and a sister who were married and older than them.

When Tom walked into the church with his parents, it was full of believers, both men and women. The priest and deacons had already started the Mass, and the smell of incense was in the place. Before Tom sat down, he closed his eyes for a moment and prayed, "Accept me, Lord. I don't deserve to taint the holiness of Your house and Your sacred secrets, but if You accept me, You will save my weak soul."

From time to time, the voices of the choir would rise with wonderful hymns from the top floor of the church. The prayers, along with the melodies and icons that lined the walls from all sides, made the believers feel the presence of God, especially the sacrament of the Holy Eucharist present on the altar. When the time came, the believers usually participated with the choir in reciting the 'Our Father' prayer, which was included in the liturgy in Syriac Aramaic, with a beautiful, sweet melody, to make the Mass truly a movement that brought us closer to God.

Following the Mass, most of the faithful gathered in the main church hall for socializing and coffee. This included Tom's sister Amalia and her children Peter and Amanda, as well as Tom's married brother Manuel, along with Manuel's wife Helene and spoiled daughter Lauren. When they met, they greeted each other. Then, the Mother approached and embraced her children and kissed her grandchildren with love and tenderness.

"Don't forget, we have a lovely excursion planned for next Saturday," Tom reminded Peter. Peter was ten years old; his sister Amanda was five, and Lauren was four.

Peter smiled and said, "I won't forget."

Then, Tom told Amanda and Lauren, "When you both are as old as Peter, I will take you both on some awesome trips and tell you about how much Jesus loves you!"

Tom then brought them some of the cake available on the refreshment table while the family members were drinking coffee. Marcus, along with Father Stephen, the parish priest, approached and greeted everyone. He had inquired of the priest about some matters related to his wedding preparations, and the priest reassured him that everything would be in order. Then, the priest asked Tom if he needed anything for the trip that he organized for the parish children, as he was responsible for them and taught them religious lessons.

Tom replied, "I've already booked a big bus for our ride and sorted out the rest of the trip stuff."

While they were talking, Maria, the catechist with Tom, sauntered over with her tall and slender figure, long chestnut hair, sun-kissed skin, and deer-like hazel eyes shaped like almonds. After greeting everyone, she sat down with them. "You're lookin' more gorgeous every day, sweetie," Tom said with dreamy eyes.

Maria smiled and lowered her head shyly. To avoid embarrassment, Tom asked her if she was ready to go on the trip with the kids. She replied, "Yes!" She and her choirmate Caroline taught the boys carols and helped Tom with pastoral activities.

Tom asked, "Do you think the boys will have a blast on this trip?"

Maria replied, "Definitely. Kids need fun, play, and visiting new places more than adults do." Everyone's face lit up as they expressed their admiration for her.

After church, the Aphram family went to the house for lunch. The Mother had previously invited them to this meal.

Meanwhile, Marcus went to pick up his fiancée, Natalie, and Mom went into the kitchen with Amalia and Helene to get lunch ready. Most of the time, Mom cooked the food the day before and put it in the fridge. Then, all she had to do was pop it in the oven and whip up a salad. Tom took care of the kids and took them to the garden to play on the swings and slides.

The house's garden was big and had green, lush grass. On either side were trimmed bushes, and near the house walls, there were beautiful flowers of various colors. The father planted them and took care of them. The house was also big, and it had two floors. The first floor had a spacious and elegant sitting room, an office, and a kitchen that opened to the dining room. On the second floor, there were four bedrooms.

When Marcus arrived with his fiancée and Amalia's husband, Adam, the food was ready. Then, everyone sat around the table. The father raised his eyes to the sky and prayed, "Lord, bless this food that You have given us, and shower us with Your never-ending gifts and blessings because we know You always have our backs. And please let us be good enough to sit at your table in Heaven someday. Amen."

They praised the Mother because of the lovely dish as they began to eat. She had prepared a platter of mashed eggplant and a platter of rice for them. Everyone lifted their glasses excitedly and made a toast to Marcus and Natalie.

One of the secrets of happiness in life is having a perfect family and good people around you. After the meal, the women cleaned up the kitchen and made tea and coffee. Then, they joined the men who were sitting out in the living room. Typically, in every gathering, Tom would select a topic for discussion. This time, his choice was 'parapsychology' or, in simpler terms, the paranormal sciences.

Tom began by saying, "Some people who study paranormal science say there is proof that telepathy and telekinesis are real, that you can move things without touching them, as well as the reality of healing through the hands of therapeutic powers. And, of course, there is no doubt that dreams are real. My question is: Do you think these things are true or just made up?"

Manuel replied, "I don't believe in these things you mentioned, except dreams. There are different types of dreams, according to my knowledge. Some are like visions from God, some are events that come before they happen, and others come from a person's mental state or even from the effect of eating a lot of food before sleeping."

Natalie raised her hand and wondered about what Manuel had said about sometimes seeing the future in our dreams. Then she asked, "How can flesh and blood show us the future? It's impossible unless there's something else in the body that's beyond matter, like the spirit. And I think the idea of seeing the future through dreams is real."

Adam interrupted and continued, "I want to touch on the topic of telepathy. If a human was like an animal that has only a soul without a spirit, telepathy would be impossible. Because the spirit has the ability to think, and since we have a breath of God's spirit within us, God's spirit can communicate with us at any time and even reside within us. We can communicate with it through our prayers, and the more we ascend in holiness and spirituality, the more we can hear His voice and respond. This is what happens with saints. We have the ability to telepathize, but it is hidden from us right now, and only a small number of people in the world can feel it. But when we die, our spirits will ascend to Heaven, where telepathy will be the main way to communicate with God, angels, and even saints and true believers."

"It makes sense from a spiritual point of view," said Tom, backing up Adam's explanation.

Helen raised her hand and asked, "Can a person move things without touching them? I can't say for sure, but I think some envious people might still be able to cause harm and damage to others, even though their power is limited these days. This is because, as Christians, we are blessed with the holy power of baptism. However, in the past, envious eyes caused a lot of harm to those around them. Let me clarify: it's not the eyes themselves that are harmful; it's the envious spirit within them. So, there are some spirits that can cause harm because they have evil powers, and there are others that can heal because they've been gifted with extraordinary healing abilities by God. However, God decides how these abilities are used, based on His wisdom and plan."

Marcus raised his hands and said sarcastically, "I'm impressed by your vision and explanation of these facts. I wanted to say the same thing, but you beat me to it."

After that, he and the others laughed together. As the guests left in the afternoon, Marcus took his fiancée for a walk before returning to her parents' house. Tom took advantage of the situation by calling Maria from his room.

"Hello, sweetie, what's up?" Tom said.

"Hello, Tom. I'm doing good," replied Maria.

"How was your day?" Tom said.

"It was awesome and fun. My dad took us out for lunch, and then we went for a walk in nature," replied Maria. "And you, how was your day?"

Tom answered, "We had a beautiful day, and the whole family enjoyed a delicious lunch together. Then, I chose to talk about parapsychology."

"Did you have different opinions about it?" asked Maria.

"Nope, everyone had similar opinions," Tom replied. "Disagreements, my love, often come from lack of knowledge and narrow-mindedness. If we have different opinions, it's important to respect and accept them until the full truth is revealed. Then, everyone can agree on the presented evidence."

"You called me 'my love.' Do you love me, Tom?" Maria inquired.

Tom replied, "Yes, I love you so much that the days I don't see or hear from you don't count in my life."

"You're a liar and are deceiving me," Maria said.

Tom replied, "I won't swear to you because swearing is wrong according to church teachings. It's enough for me to say that I truly love you; your love is like the soul that gives life to the body."

Maria asked, "Am I that important to you in this way?"

Tom replied, "Yeah, even more than that, my love. By the way, tomorrow at the end of university, I'll take you out to lunch."

Maria said, "Okay."

Tom said, "All right, see you soon, my beauty."

Maria said, "See you later, chatty. Haha."

Their love blossomed two years ago when Maria began accompanying her mother to church, and it grew stronger as she became involved in the choir and helped the parish children. Her mother was of Syriac-Aramaic descent, while her father was an American of Spanish descent. Likewise, Tom's people were Syriac-Aramaic and committed to their church, which preserved their faith and identity.

Tom was raised in a religious environment. He was inclined to spirituality. Therefore, he was able to continue and follow his church's service. He had good qualities, such as calmness, sensitivity, and a joyful spirit. He was also handsome, with a fair complexion, dark eyes, an average height, and a slim body. He found in Maria the qualities that he dreamed of in a woman—she was gentle, kind, humble, and faithful.

These unique and amazing traits enchanted him, just like a moth drawn to light. He loved her, and she felt the same way. A surge of happiness would wash over him whenever his eyes met hers, which were shining with the sparkle of magic and longing. Lights danced, a sweet scent filled the air, and the colors all around him dazzled as he stood in front of her, feeling love course through his veins like blood.

Night fell, and the stars spread out their blanket across the clear sky, with the shining moon in the center. At this time, Tom usually liked to do his favorite hobbies, like reading a book or listening to music. He loved reading spiritual and romantic books in spite of not enjoying studying. He left it behind when he finished high school, but he continued to read. As for music, he liked peaceful songs and sometimes lively songs if their rhythm was beautiful.

Tom had a positive nature, and his heart was filled with love, so he was concerned with helping others if they needed him. He had a strong relationship with God, as he raised his prayers to Him every night, eagerly and humbly, asking that God's mercy and grace would be upon all humanity and that love and peace would be planted in their hearts.

In the morning, Tom got up as usual, made his breakfast, and then sat in the garden for a while. He enjoyed sitting in the garden early in the morning when it was still cool. The serene surroundings and peaceful environment had an indelible impact on him, providing him with a sense of relaxation and peace. Tom got into his pickup truck and drove to work when it was time to start his job. Tom and his brother Manuel worked in their father's lumber store, while their other brother, Marcus, was a self-employed architect.

Tom's father had immigrated with his family to this area thirty years ago. He had worked at this store for a long time, and when the owner offered it for sale due to health reasons, his father was able to take a loan from the bank and bought it. Tom's father had retired, but he still came from time to time and supervised them and two other employees. Their wood sales increased, especially in the spring and summer, and this indicated good management and treatment in the store.

Tom told Manuel that he had to leave to take Maria to a restaurant for lunch. Then he got into his car and drove to the university. When he arrived there, Maria was waiting for him. She got into the car and greeted him:

"Hey, Tom!"

"Hi, my princess. How was university today?" Tom asked.

"I'm tired of all the lectures," Maria said.

Tom said, "I'm going to let you get rid of this boredom with a bomb meal that'll make you forget all about university stress."

Tom turned the car toward the parking lot of one of the restaurants. Then he and Maria got out and sat outside, as the weather was beautiful. The waiter came and served them two glasses of refreshing drinks. And after that, they ordered two delicious meals.

While waiting for the lunch to be ready, Maria said, "My friend at the university told me today that her parents divorced after twenty-five years of marriage. She was bummed, and I felt sad for her. How could they separate after such a long time?"

"I guess the foundation their marriage was built on wasn't

solid, so over time, it started to crack," Tom answered.

"But how?" Maria asked.

"The reasons are different," Tom said, "but they all come from the same source, which is love. Love is both the problem and the solution. For example, a young man may meet a beautiful girl, fall in love, and marry. Both have the same level of competence, professionally and socially. Then, after a while of being married, it becomes clear that the husband loves his wife thirty percent and loves himself seventy percent, while the wife loves her husband seventy percent and loves herself thirty percent. Here, we can see that the husband's love for his wife is negative and selfish, whereas the wife's love for her husband is positive. They keep getting into fights mainly because their love for each other isn't equal, and neither of them realizes it.

"In most cases, this conflict leads to infidelity or divorce in developed societies. However, in poor and religious countries, women often bear the burden and sacrifice themselves for their children or for the sake of reputation because they will tarnish their family name or have no family at all if they get divorced. It should be noted that this refers to the majority, not everyone, and that in most cases, the woman is the one who sacrifices."

Tom continued, "In the system of love, there is an exchange of emotions. If it flows from one side without the other, the system will change after some time, and daily conflicts will arise. I know both sides bear the consequences of mistakes, as humans are imperfect. But when there is true mutual love, both sides will sacrifice for each other to maintain and harmonize their relationship."

Maria said, "Yeah, that's the truth, but where'd you get all this information from?"

"From the books I've read and the divorce cases going on around us, my dear," he stated.

Maria asked, "After living together for a long time, will you leave me?"

"If you love me more than yourself, I won't leave you," Tom replied.

Tom smiled, held her hand, looked into her eyes, and said, "I feel that the huge amount of love we share every moment flows through our hearts." And then he kissed her hand. Then the waiter came with the food, and Tom said jokingly, "Enough talking about love; when the food arrives at the door, love runs out of the window."

In a playful tone, Maria asked him, "Do you want me to be a good cook after marriage, or do you want me to be your lover who wanders with you?"

He replied, "Both, my love, for the balance will be as complete as possible."

They both laughed, and Maria added, "What about my future dreams?"

He laughed and then said, "I'm just teasing you; of course, it's natural for us to cooperate in household matters, especially if you want to work."

After they finished their meal, he told her, "I have a surprise for you; my birthday is coming up this Saturday."

She replied, "I know that my dear, and I have a special gift for you."

He asked, "What is it?"

She replied, "Let's keep it a surprise until the time comes."

He said, "Okay, next Saturday night, we'll go out together to one of the best restaurants with Marcus and Natalie, but before that, we have a trip with the church's children."

Maria agreed without hesitation, and after their conversation ended, Tom took her to her parents' house.

Chapter Two

The days passed quickly until Saturday morning when the kids gathered in front of the church with their guides. Maria wore a light purple blouse and jeans, and she tied her hair with a colorful headband. Tom greeted her in the morning, saying, "You always look elegant and beautiful, my dear."

Mary smiled and thanked him, saying, "No need for flattery now."

The bus arrived, everyone got on it, and they headed to the most beautiful place in the area, Griffith Park and Observatory. The weather was suitable for this enjoyable trip. At the beginning of the journey, the kids started singing songs and hymns that they loved until they reached their destination. Everyone went to the park, where there was a big observatory on a hill with a view of the pretty city of Burbank.

The boys were amazed by its size and beauty, so they went with the guide who was waiting for them in the square to tell them about the observatory and the strange things inside. In the beginning, he mentioned that this large land was once the property of a wealthy lord named Jenkins Griffith, and in 1933, he brought the best telescope at that time and looked at the sky one evening. He was impressed by the sights he saw and decided to fund the construction of a planetarium and a large observatory on this mountain, which was called Mount Hollywood and was designed by the architect John Austin.

In 1935, the project was completed, and the observatory and

planetarium shows were ready. The observatory and park were named after the owner and funder (Griffith) as a tribute to and permanent recognition of him.

After that, the children went into the building, and the guide told them about an important job in the observatory. They saw many pictures of space and a small model of some of the planets hanging from the ceiling in the big hall. The boys were surprised to see old and new telescopes and stones of different sizes from a meteorite. Then, as they went by the big observatory hall, the boys' faces lit up with excitement. They were very interested in what they were seeing and hearing. After the guide had finished explaining, everyone went outside. Tom led the boys to a quiet place where they could sit and eat.

Tom said to them, "You have an hour to eat and rest. After that, we have a spiritual topic to talk about. Then you can play as much as you want until it's time to go back." Then, the children cheered happily.

"I think this visit will leave a beautiful impact on the boys' hearts," Tom said as he sat near Maria.

"I agree, this is a truly special trip. I'm enjoying it too. How about you?" Maria replied.

"Everything I see and hear is beautiful and affects me as long as I'm with you," Tom said. "While I was inside, I wished that I could take you to a planet like Earth and build you a big palace by the sea surrounded by the most beautiful gardens and roses, and both of us would live in it."

"Wow, what a great romantic dream!" Maria said. "But thanks, I don't want such a big palace because I'll get bored of it after a month. I want to see people around me and live with those I love and who love me, and, of course, you're the first one. I'm happy just to live with you in a simple house. This is the kind of perfect life I want to live, my love."

Tom said, "I will prepare a spaceship that will take you anywhere at the speed of light whenever you want."

"Keep it for the honeymoon," she replied jokingly.

"You got me this time." Tom laughed.

Maria and Tom had brought some snacks and placed them on the table. Then their colleague Caroline came and joined them as well. Tom called his nephew Peter to come and eat with them, and Tom had also brought some juice and some soft drinks with him. After the mealtime was over, everyone sat around Tom so he could tell them a story about the prodigal son found in the Bible.

He said, "Once upon a time, there was a wealthy man with two sons whom he loved deeply. One day, the younger son said to his father, 'Father, I want my share of the inheritance because I want to go to a different country and live there.'

"The father tried to discourage his son from leaving, but he couldn't change his mind. So, he reluctantly gave him his share of the inheritance. After that, the younger son left his father and brother and migrated to another country.

"After having fun with his money there, he slowly spent it all until he had nothing left. During that time, a famine hit the country, and the younger son tried to find a job to alleviate his hunger. Finally, he found a job, but in a pigsty. He agreed to work there in exchange for the food they were giving him, which was just a few pods that barely filled him up. This type of food was given to the pigs.

"He felt very sorry for himself and thought, *My father has many hired servants and has plenty of bread left, and here I am starving. I'll go to him and tell him, 'As a result of my sin against heaven and against you, I'm not worthy of being your son any more. Make me like one of your hired servants.'*

"After he got up and left the barn to go to his father, the father saw him and had compassion for him. He hugged and kissed him, and the son said, 'Father, I have sinned against heaven and against you. I am not worthy to be called your son, but let me be one of your servants.'

"The father told his servants, 'Get the finest robe for him and put it on him. Put a ring on his finger and sandals on his feet and slaughter the fatted calf for him so we can eat and be happy because this son of mine was dead and is now alive again. He got lost, but now he is found.'

"When his oldest son got back from working in the field, he heard music and dancing, so he asked one of the servants, 'What's going on?'

"The servant replied, 'Your brother came back, and your father slaughtered the fatted calf for him because he had returned safely.'

"Due to his anger, the eldest son did not enter the house, so his father went out to speak with him. The son said, 'Look! All these years, I've been slaving for you and never disobeyed your orders. Yet you never gave me even a young goat so I could celebrate with my friends. But when this son of yours, who has squandered your property with prostitutes, came home, you slaughtered the fattened calf for him!'

"'My son,' the father said, 'you are always with me, and everything I have is yours. But we had to celebrate and be glad because your brother was dead and is alive again; he was lost and is found.'"

After telling the story, Tom asked the kids, "What can we learn from this amazing story?"

Matthias, one of the children, raised his hand, saying,

"Repent. When we think in a wrong way and fall into a problem, it's best to repent and return to what we were on."

Tom agreed with Matthias and said, "Right, that's a great lesson we can learn from this story."

Peter raised his hand and said, "Repentance. When we do something stupid and hurt someone else and later realize our mistake, it's not enough to just feel sorry; we must apologize and ask for forgiveness from the person we wronged."

Tom said, "That's also great, Peter. That is a good answer and explanation. In this case, we must be courageous because someone who asks for forgiveness from someone they have wronged is a brave person."

James, one of the boys, raised his hand and said, "This story is about love. If a father does not love his son, he will not forgive him."

Tom agreed with James and said, "Certainly, James. Love is the root of all that is good and right. We are nothing without love. Love gives value and meaning to our lives. Well done, James."

Then Caroline jumped in, "I see in this parable a model for the Jews and the nations. All of them are 'the children of God the Father,' so simply because 'the Father' invited the nations that strayed into sin to repent, giving them ownership of the heavens, the Jews distanced themselves from Him. Is this true?"

Tom said, "There's no doubt that all the prophecies in the Torah and other Old Testament books about the coming of the Messiah were fulfilled when Jesus Christ, the second Hypostasis of the Trinity, came and took on a physical body. At that time, the Jews didn't recognize Christ because they believed that 'the Messiah' would come with power and might, freeing them from Roman occupation and establishing his rule over all the land that God had promised their father, Abraham. However, he came in the opposite way: poor, humble, loving both the righteous and the sinners, and showing compassion toward the occupying Romans, so they rejected him. But there is hope for their return because the saintly apostle Paul prophesied the end times."

After Tom had finished speaking, the kids went to play. Caroline was watching the boys as Tom and Maria went toward the place that overlooked the city of Burbank and the green Sierra mountains. There was something magical about the view.

As he was moving a strand of her hair out of her eyes, he said, "I wrote something beautiful for you, and I would like to read it to you so it can stay as a memory in this place we're standing in." He picked up a piece of paper and read: "Since the first time I laid eyes on you, your sweet and enchanting smile has seeped deep into my heart, lifting me to a world more beautiful and wonderful than dreams and imagination. How can I escape from you when your eyes have captured me in this amazing and unique world, and I no longer want to leave it? Your love has become the air I breathe and the life I live."

As his words touched her heart, her eyes sparkled. She fell into his arms and whispered, "I heard the most beautiful and wonderful words that shook me from the inside out."

He replied, "You will always hear more as long as you stay close to me."

Following that, they took some pictures together and with other people to remember the trip. After the trip was over, Tom, Maria, and Caroline got the kids back on the bus, and everyone was happy to come home after this fun and memorable experience.

In the evening, Tom got ready and put on stylish clothes that fit his birthday celebration. Then, he went to his car to accompany Maria to the restaurant. Then Tom rang the doorbell, and her mother opened the door and welcomed him.

Maria's parents loved Tom because their daughter always described him as gentle and noble. The moment Maria heard the doorbell, she walked out of her room. When Tom saw her, he was impressed by her pretty face, which she had lightly adorned with makeup, her elegant burgundy dress, and her long, sparkling hair.

He told her, "You are not only beautiful today, but you are also charming."

After she thanked him for this touching compliment, he asked her parents if they could go out together. When they got to the restaurant, Marcus and Natalie were there to greet them. After that, everyone went to the table that Tom had reserved ahead of time.

"The night is special for me because I'm saying goodbye to a year and hello to a new one," Tom said.

"How old are you going to be?" Natalie asked.

"Twenty-four years old," Tom replied.

"What are your plans for the coming year?" Marcus asked.

"Exciting news, Maria and I have decided to get married after a year, around this time," Tom replied.

"It's great news! I'm thrilled to hear it," Marcus said. "I hope that God makes your happy wish come true."

"Thank you for this beautiful prayer," Tom said.

"After the wedding, where do you and Natalie want to spend your honeymoon?" asked Maria.

"Near the beaches of Malibu," Marcus replied.

"It's amazing. It's a beautiful tourist spot. I hope that you both will have a great time there," Maria said.

Marcus and Natalie said, "Thank you."

"Cheers to Tom and Maria's happiness," Marcus said as he raised his glass.

Tom raised his glass, too, and said, "Cheers to you."

Then, everyone drank. Tom asked them, "What is happiness?" Instead of waiting for an answer from anyone, Tom answered his own question by saying, "It is when a person can find a balance between what the body and mind require of thought, and specifically what the soul and spirit require in achieving their goals by enacting and achieving them. If a person is able, according to his capabilities, to fulfill these wishes, he will have achieved the happiness he aspires to."

Markus said, "We thank God for making it easier for us to find happiness, especially with the love of these two wonderful girls."

"That's true because love is one of the most important things that leads to happiness, but there are other things you need to be truly happy, too, like health, financial security, and ambition," Tom said.

Natalie said, "Yeah, there are a bunch of things that must be in place to reach total happiness."

As the loud music got louder, everyone stood up and went to the dance floor, where they danced until they were exhausted. Tom had ordered a cake from the restaurant, and the waiter brought it over and lit twenty-four candles.

"Before the candles are blown out, Tom, make a wish in your heart," Marcus said.

"I hope Maria will be with me," Tom said. "I pray to God that our only wish, which is to get married, will come true."

Maria smiled and nodded her head in agreement, and then Tom blew out the candles.

Markus and Natalie said, "Happy birthday! Wishing you all the best." Maria also wished him a happy birthday.

After eating the cake, they got up and danced again, but this time, it was a slow dance. As they danced to the music, Tom asked Maria to close her eyes because he wanted to bring back some of the happy memories they had shared together. He whispered to her about some of the beautiful memories that had left a big impact on both of their hearts. Then he took her with him to a beautiful place: a land filled with green grass and a clear lake with two white swans swimming in it. There was a gathering of families, friends, and a priest at the altar waiting to wed them. Maria's burgundy dress became a white wedding gown, and as she approached the altar with her groom, large bouquets of roses filled the place.

When the priest wedded them, rainbow-colored petals fell from the sky. Kisses, dances, and joy were shared between the bride and the groom. When Maria opened her eyes in the restaurant hall, she was so happy that her eyes filled with tears of joy. After looking at Tom and hugging him tightly, Maria and Tom went back to their seats while Marcus and Natalie kept dancing.

Maria gave him a luxurious watch for his birthday, which he liked and thanked her for. Everyone went home after having a good time at the restaurant. But before they left, Maria gave Tom a kiss that was more valuable than the first gift she gave him.

Chapter Three

The great day finally came: Natalie and Marcus' wedding. The ladies donned their most stunning gowns and hairdos while the guys suited up in new black suits, white shirts, and bold, colorful ties.

Everyone gathered inside and outside the church until the beautifully decorated wedding car arrived with its flowers and colored ribbons. The women cheered happily, and then the bride's father took her hand and walked with her to present her to her groom, Marcus.

They entered the church, which was decorated with flowers and white and blue ribbons, and stood in front of the altar with Tom and Maria close by. The priest then started the wedding ceremony. There were cries of joy and excitement during the ceremony, especially when the priest placed crowns on the bride's and groom's heads. At the end of the prayer, the priest blessed them, and then the couple's families gathered to accept the congratulations and take some memorable photos with them.

The invitees gathered in a large hall, which had been prepared for wedding ceremonies, near the church. It was decorated and arranged in a beautiful way that impressed the guests. Round tables were laid out in the middle of the hall, and each table seated ten people. The tables were draped in gold fabrics, each one adorned by a large vase of white roses. A candle was placed between these roses. Translucent curtains in a variety of light colors covered the walls on all sides of the hall. Many people were waiting for the newlyweds to arrive, and the band and singer were ready to greet them.

When the bride and groom entered the hall, everyone cheered and clapped to the beat of drums, lutes, and cheerful music. Then, the bride and groom danced, and the guests stood around and clapped until the music got quieter. Everyone took their seat, and Tom and Maria sat near the bride and groom in the hall's front row.

Thereafter, most of the guests had their meal, and then the musicians began singing exciting and joyful Syriac songs, so the guests and family began dancing with the newlyweds until they became exhausted. Then, a waiter brought a multi-tiered cake into the hall, where some of the guests joined the bride and groom to help cut it. After everyone had eaten a piece of cake, they stood up again to dance with the newlyweds, this time to quiet instruments.

Tom grabbed Maria's hand and started swaying to the music. He leaned in and whispered in her ear, "Next year, at this exact time, we'll be tying the knot too. Ain't it just amazing to think about becoming each other's?"

"Certainly, it's our beloved dream that we hope to fulfill," she replied.

He wanted to hug and kiss her, but they were in front of a lot of people who were watching them. The party went on until late at night in a joyful and happy atmosphere. Guests congratulated the newlyweds, presented them with gifts, and wished them well. The newlyweds bid their family and friends farewell and left for their honeymoon at dawn.

A week after the wedding, the joyful news of the newlyweds had spread to both the Aphram and Shimon families, which Tom was happy to share with Maria each evening. During one of their calls, Maria told Tom that she had one month left to finish her studies in business administration and said to him, "I will apply for a job at the bank where my father works."

"I think it's fine because you have always liked this kind of work and become knowledgeable at it. Good luck," Tom said.

Maria applied for a job at the bank two days later, then met her father in his office. It had been twenty-five years since her father worked at this bank. His career progressed through a number of positions until he was promoted to be the manager. The proud father greeted his daughter and told her she would get a job when she finished studying.

As Maria drank coffee in her father's office, Mr. Walter, the owner of the bank, entered and welcomed them. He was a young man in the spring of his life. Maria's father introduced the bank owner to her, saying, "This is Mr. Walter, the bank owner."

Then he said to Mr. Walter, "This is my daughter, Maria." They greeted each other, and then she sat down again. She could guess from the way he looked at her that he was impressed with her.

"Today, my daughter filled out an employment application with us," her father told Mr. Walter.

"I think she'll get the job because we need someone as beautiful as her in the bank," the young man replied. Then he added: "By the way, I'd like to invite both of you to lunch at the nearby restaurant."

The father and daughter agreed. Then Mr. Walter left. Maria was surprised because Mr. Walter was the bank owner despite his young age.

Her father replied, "He inherited it from his father and grandfather. Sadly, his father passed away two years ago and left him a hefty inheritance as the only heir to the family fortune."

When lunchtime rolled around, they met up at the restaurant. Mr. Walter asked Maria about her qualifications, and she told him that she had studied business administration. Then he asked her another question: "What makes a person successful in his profession?"

She answered, "Love for the profession and passion lead a person to success and creativity in it."

Mr. Walter expressed his admiration after that and told her, "Congratulations, you got the job, and you can start as soon as you get the certificate."

"Thank you for the job, and thank you for your great trust in me," Maria said.

In the evening, Maria was very happy, and she called Tom and told him about what had happened, and he was happy.

"This is a happy occasion; we should celebrate it," Tom said.

"Yeah, go ahead and pick a restaurant that you like, and I'll invite you," Maria said.

"I won't put it off. Let's meet tomorrow after university," Tom said, laughing.

"All right, troublemaker," Maria said.

The next day, they met up at a restaurant and were so happy to be with each other, as if they were two little kids.

"Once I get a job, I'll save most of my salary to help us reach our goal. After we get married, I would like to have a beautiful house surrounded by a garden, where I can take care of the flowers and bushes all the time, and two wonderful children to take care of and pamper," said Maria.

Suddenly, Tom said, "And who will pamper and take care of me?"

"It's too late for you, my old child," Maria said while laughing loudly. Then they both laughed.

"If the days keep making us laugh, I will make our dreams come true. We will take care of our two children until they become young men, and when they get married, I will buy a beautiful house near a beach to spend the rest of our days in, listening to the sound of the waves and sleeping to their melodies," Tom said.

"I also love the sea, my love," Maria said.

Tom and Maria had some good days, and they were optimistic about realizing their pink dream, which had almost come true. Since their souls connected before their physical bodies did, nothing or nobody could ever tear them apart from now on.

Chapter Four

One evening, Maria's father sat in the living room and called his wife and daughter over. With a heavy heart, he said to them, "I have something I need to talk about. As you know, I work as a bank manager, and a part of my job is to keep an eye on the stock market. I've been steadily buying and trading stocks for a while now, and I ended up buying a ton of them. Unfortunately, their value took a major dive yesterday. The bad news is that I borrowed most of the money to buy them from the bank, and I won't be able to pay it back no matter how hard I work for the rest of my life."

While he was talking, tears were streaming down his face, and he continued, "The worst thing is, when I took out this big loan, I had to fudge some documents because the requirements didn't match up with my situation. The bank owner can imprison me for what I did, but when Mr. Walter found out, he came up with a suggestion after giving it some thought. He proposes to marry Maria as a way of turning a blind eye to my wrongdoing and forgetting about the money lost on the stock market."

Maria cried after hearing this. Her dad looked at her with sadness and said, "Think about what's best for you, my daughter. I won't make you do anything you don't want to."

Maria left her dad and went to her room, crying. What is this? It's a disaster. Suddenly, all the dreams she had with Tom over the past two years fell apart in front of her. She was shocked and didn't know if she was awake or if a nightmare was taking over her body and mind. She couldn't sleep all night and felt lost.

That night, Tom dreamed that he was on the roof of a skyscraper, and he was holding the edge, but his hands slipped, and he fell down to the bottom. He woke up from the shock. Then he made a sign of the cross on his chest and whispered, "Dear God, I am feeling anxious and uneasy. Please comfort me with Your presence and help me to find peace. I know that You are always with me, and I trust in Your love and protection. Please protect me from any harm or evil that may be associated with this dream."

The next day, Maria didn't go to the university. Instead, she stayed in her room all day, feeling sad and hopeless and unable to decide what to do. She called Tom after he finished work and told him, "We need to meet."

He could hear the sadness and worry in her voice and asked her, "What's wrong?"

She couldn't answer; she just cried. He said to her, "Okay, we'll meet."

After a few minutes, he came and picked her up from home, and they sat in a café. The sun was still sending its rays, which had started to fade gradually and turn into shining reddish and purplish colors in the sky.

She told him all about what had happened with her dad and the price she would pay in exchange. She said, "I've been feeling pretty low, both mentally and physically, since yesterday."

He responded, "We don't have any chance, sweetheart. The matter is settled. We weren't born to live a happy life but to sacrifice for others. That's just how it goes."

She cried in his arms, and he cried, too, before taking her back to her home. That night, Tom got down on his knees in front of the crucified Jesus Christ in his room and prayed with all his heart, "Lord, before I met Maria, my love and passion were to devote myself to You. You already know that I wanted to be a monk. But I was waiting for a sign from You to show that You were calling me to this holy mission. When I didn't get a sign, I thought You wanted me to stay in the world I was in, to be a better person, and to have a righteous Christian family.

"With Maria, I found peace and joy. I also found my other half, the person who makes me whole and happy. To what end will my Maria be assumed by someone else? You know my devotion and love for You and how I have served You and will continue to serve You. I pray, my Lord, to bring her back to me and take this cup away from me. But if this is what you want, I will bear this heavy cross and accept it respectfully for You."

Days passed, and the burden grew heavier. Neither Maria nor Tom had any hope of finding relief from their suffering, and communication had stopped between them. Meanwhile, while Tom and Manuel were working in the store, their father called and told them that their brother Marcus and his wife Natalie had been in an accident on their way back from their honeymoon.

They closed the store and ran over when he told them the hospital address. Driving to the hospital took about an hour. After the first aid and exams, the doctors put Marcus and Natalie in the ICU because their condition was still critical. When they arrived, their family was terrified and sobbing.

Tom had to go home at midnight to get a few hours of sleep so he could run the store in the morning. When he got home, he kneeled before the crucifix again and prayed, "God, please save my brother and his wife from this danger and heal them. I know You have the power and control over everything. Maria is dear to me, and I sacrificed her love for Your sake. I beg You; please save their lives in honor of this sacrifice and my service to You and the Church."

Early in the morning, he received a call from his older brother, Manuel, informing him that Marcus had passed away. When Tom heard those words, he felt like he was hit by a bolt of lightning. It was as if the world had gone dark in his eyes, and he wished he had died instead of Marcus.

Marcus' body was placed in a coffin in front of the altar a week later. Relatives and friends flocked to console them. The church was filled with mourners wearing black clothes. The sounds of sobbing could be heard from time to time as the priest conducted the funeral ceremony. Following that, he stood on the pulpit and delivered a condolence speech, saying:

"In such circumstances, it is difficult for the priest to offer comfort to the deceased's family because there are no appropriate words that can take away their sadness and replace it with patience and consolation.

"I recently read a beautiful story about grief, and I'd like to share it with you so that we can find some solace in the reasons for these painful events. There was a family who had only one son. One day, he got sick and died. A lot of people came to offer their condolences, and one of them told the father, 'Adam had two sons, and one of them killed the other. But Adam turned to God only for comfort.'

"'What do I have to do with Adam and his kids?' the father replied.

"Then another mourner stood up and said, 'Job had many sons and daughters and possessions, but he lost everything because of Satan's temptation, but he turned to God only for comfort.'

"'What do I have to do with Job?' the father replied.

"The third mourner said, 'Someone was going to another

country, and he didn't want to take something valuable with him. He turned to his friend and said, "I'll leave this valuable thing with you, and when I come back, I'll get it back."

"'In response, his friend said, "I'll keep your deposit."

"'Time passed, days and years, and one day that man returned and visited his friend and asked about his deposit, and his friend replied, "I promised to keep it, and here it is…"'

"The mourner continued his speech and said, 'When God blesses people with sons and daughters, he has entrusted them with these valuable gifts, and we cannot ask Him why He wants to take them from us.'

"The father of the deceased was moved by this example and said, 'Truly, I found comfort in your words.'"

In his last words, the priest told everyone that Natalie had been taken out of intensive care and was slowly getting better.

There, at the cemetery, the family of Marcus bade him farewell at his final resting place and felt that they had lost a part of themselves. Maria and her family were among the people who came to offer their sympathy to the Aphram family. The rest of the Aphram family and their friends went back to the church hall to eat a mercy meal for the departed spirit.

After two months, Tom was still under the weight of shock and in a spiral, he couldn't get out of, especially after hearing about Maria's wedding. At the time, he dreamed that she was standing in front of the church in a wedding dress. She would look back, hoping that her lover would come back and save her. Since then, Tom has stopped going to church and going anywhere else except for work. All the places he visited in the area reminded him of her: restaurants, cafes, stores, and even the streets.

The priest paid a visit to the Aphram family and requested to speak with Tom alone to persuade him to return to the church.

The priest said to him, "You know, my son, that Christ didn't promise believers an easy life on earth. Instead, He warned us and showed us that there are difficulties we must overcome and crosses we must bear. He also said in the Gospel: 'Enter through the narrow gate. For wide is the gate, and broad is the road that leads to destruction, and many enter through it. But small is the gate and narrow the road that leads to life, and only a few find it.'"

Tom said, "Since I was a child, I have been with the Lord. I follow His commandments and have worked for Him in His house. If He wanted me to go to the monastery, I would have done it gladly and offered myself as a sacrifice for Him. But when I needed Him during this time, He did not help me or answer my prayers. Instead, He abandoned me in despair and hopelessness."

Then he added, "This made me wonder a lot of things, like, why does the life of a righteous person fail on this earth, but the life of an evil one succeeds? Why is the right of the poor usurped and given to someone else? Why does God allow spirits that love each other to be separated?"

The priest cut him off and said, "I understand, there are questions we cannot easily answer, but there is no question without an answer because Christ says to the believers, 'Ask and it will be given to you; seek and you will find; knock and the door will be opened for you.'"

Tom replied, "Okay, I'll look for answers until I find them, even if it takes the rest of my life."

The priest left him with the hope that he would return to the church again. That night, Tom thought to himself, *How can I keep looking for answers to my questions while also making some money for my living?* Tom stayed up all night thinking until he found a solution.

First of all, he had to get out of the vortex that ravaged his mind and heart by moving away from the area that reminded him of Maria.

Secondly, he needed to choose a place devoid of people so he could read and reflect to reach his answers.

Thirdly, he needed to secure an income that would allow him to live.

The next day, Tom bought a newspaper and searched for a job on one of the remote farms until he found one. He contacted the advertiser and agreed with him on everything. The farm was located in a place called Valley Springs in Calaveras.

One night, Tom sat down with his parents and told them that he was going to work on a farm far away for a while to heal from his wounds. Tom's dad said, "We need you more than ever, son. Your being here comforts us and makes up for the loss of your brother. But, since you're going through a tough time mentally and can't seem to snap out of it, I'm blessing you and hoping that someday you'll come back to us, all healed and good as new." Then, Tom leaned over and kissed his parents' hands.

The whole family gathered at the house for his farewell. Tears were rolling down silently and passionately. The boys went over to Tom and hugged him, and Peter said, "Promise us you'll come see us on Christmas."

"I promise I'll bring you guys gifts you'll love," Tom replied.

"We don't want gifts; we just want you to be with us on Christmas," Peter said.

Tom hugged him again, and a tear fell down from his eye. Then, Manuel took him to the train station after saying goodbye.

Chapter Five

At the station, Tom said goodbye to his brother and hopped onto the train with his suitcase. He plopped down on a seat by the window and pulled out a little Sony Walkman cassette player from his pocket. He turned it on to listen to some chill music while the train began to leave the station.

Music had always been a big part of his life. He thought it had a sweet connection not only to himself but also to his soul since it set his imagination free whenever he listened to it alone. Here he was, in his imagination, returning to a time when he and his family lived in warmth, love, and contentment. He recalled the camping trips he used to take with his brothers in the mountains. It was then that he remembered how he had met Maria, fallen in love with her, started dating her, and visited amazing places with her. His mind flashed back to a time when everything was bright and happy, but now it was a tragedy he could not stand.

He remembered when she left him crying, the day his brother was buried, and visiting the cemeteries while the rain was pouring down heavily. He also remembered the dream in which he saw Maria in her wedding dress in front of the church door seeking him, but she couldn't find him.

In between reflecting on these memories and listening to music, Tom reached Valley Springs. After he got off the train, he went to the farmer who was waiting for him. They shook hands and got to know each other. Mr. Johnson had a smiling face, and he was of medium height and stout build. He seemed to be of retirement age.

Tom got into Mr. Johnson's car, and they headed toward the farm. On the way, Mr. Johnson told Tom a little bit about the farm. Mr. Johnson had two pieces of land. On one, he planted the corn, and on the other, he let his cows graze. He had ten cows, which gave him meat and milk. Before they arrived at the farm, Tom saw a calm, beautiful lake. The farmer told Tom that they lived on its banks, and it was called New Hogan Lake.

A dog barked to greet them when they arrived and got out of the car. The farmer said to Tom, "This is our friendly dog, Lucky."

Tom petted and played with Lucky for a few moments before saying, "We'll be friends, Lucky." Lucky wagged his tail. Mr. Johnson, Tom, and Lucky made their way to an old two-story house.

Mrs. Johnson had prepared dinner. The farmer introduced Tom to Mrs. Johnson, and she greeted him warmly and said, "Come have dinner with us, son."

As they began to eat, Mr. Johnson said, "We have a son who lives near New York. He studied journalism, and now he works at a newspaper. He doesn't want to come back and work on the farm. I'm getting old and need someone energetic to help me with the farm work."

Tom answered, "I really enjoy living and working in a rural environment. I have a simple and calm lifestyle."

Mr. Johnson said, "Cool, so we agreed. You'll be like our son. I'll hook you up with a place to stay next to the house, complete with a kitchen and bathroom. But we will be pleased if you share lunch and dinner with us."

Tom thanked Mr. and Mrs. Johnson for their kindness and

hospitality. After drinking tea, Mr. Johnson took Tom to his room. Tom saw that the room, kitchen, and bathroom suited him, but they needed a fresh coat of paint. He put his clothes that he brought with him in the closet and placed his books on the shelves attached to the wall. He made a deal with a bookseller in Burbank that every week, a new book on philosophical, spiritual, or religious topics would be sent to him because he was determined to find answers to his questions. Here in the countryside, he had enough time to devote himself to studying and contemplation, as he had planned.

The next day, Tom woke up at dawn, just like he always did, and put the teapot on the stove to boil water. He then opened the fridge and found it was filled with food. He selected what he needed for breakfast and placed it on the table. After eating, he put on his clothes and stepped outside to take a look around.

Lucky, the dog, approached him, wagging his tail, and Tom patted him and said, "Come on, let's go explore the area."

Tom saw a large barn for the cows, and in front of it was a big green yard. He entered the barn, and on one side, he saw a big machine with plastic tubes that were used to milk the cows. On the other side was a coop for chickens and ducks with their chicks. Close to the barn was a spacious warehouse with a tractor and farming equipment for planting and harvesting. Then he walked toward the cultivated fields and saw a whole acre of ripe corn. It was harvesting time. Nearby, there was a large and beautiful lake, and Tom was pleased when he saw it. He sat by the lake and felt a sense of happiness and relaxation.

He wondered if this place could help him forget his sadness and heal his wounds. The sun rose over the hills, so Tom walked back to the barn, where he met Mr. Johnson, dressed in his work clothes. They wished each other a good morning.

"I'll show you how I begin my day on the farm," Mr. Johnson told Tom. "First, I turn on the milk machine to get milk from the cows. Then, I take them out to the pasture to graze. Lastly, I opened the coop's door so the chickens and ducks could come out. I make sure to clean their areas to prevent diseases and keep the barn tidy."

Mr. Johnson also showed Tom how to use and operate the milk machine, as well as where to store the milk from the cows. Before lunch, Tom made sure to thoroughly clean the stable. After lunch, Mr. Johnson prepared the tractor for harvest and taught Tom how to harvest corn. After two days of hard work, the harvest was over. Mr. Johnson asked the corn merchant to send a truck to transport the crop to his large warehouses. He was impressed with and grew fond of his new worker because he was energetic, quick, and easy to teach.

At first, Tom was so exhausted from the hard work that he could hardly keep his eyes open in the evenings and would fall asleep as soon as he hit the bed. His body had not yet gotten used to this new kind of hard work. However, as time went on, he got his strength back and got used to living on a farm. He had some extra time on his hands, so he asked the farmer to buy the things he would need to paint the big house and his own room. Mr. Johnson liked Tom's idea to paint both the big house and his own room.

He bought all the paint and supplies Tom needed, as well as some wallpaper for the inside of the house. Within two weeks, the house was restored to its former luster, both inside and outside. So, Mr. and Mrs. Johnson were very happy and thanked him for all his hard work and good behavior.

Tom was able to get back to reading, thinking, and writing once his body and mind were back to their normal condition. He started writing down his memories for the first time. He started with his childhood and ended when he moved to the farm. He talked about many things and remembered both happy and sad times. In the conclusion of his memories, he wrote:

"Maria, I often miss you terribly. A longing inside me storms and scatters me like the remains of a ship on your shores. Although, I escaped from the place that reminds me of you, your fragrance still follows me, and I sense the power of your love flowing through my veins. Every day, I hear dozens of calls from your soul in the form of gentle whispers in my dreams and waking moments. Although, fate was able to destroy our hopes and dreams and keep us apart from each other, neither time nor place can extinguish the flame of our love, as our spirits became one on the day we fell in love. After losing you, I shunned life and devoted myself to researching and loving you. My soul will not accept any love except yours."

Between reading and writing, he would sit by the lake and contemplate for a while, then call his family, asking about them and reassuring them of his condition.

In December of the same year, Mr. Johnson's son surprised his parents with a visit, which was a wonderful gift for them. In celebration of this happy occasion, the parents hoped that their son Patrick would marry a girl from the countryside, but he had other dreams and plans. Their son was tall, attractive, slim, and blond. He was socially ambitious and active, and he got his morals and values from his parents.

As soon as Patrick met Tom, they became friends. In the evenings, Patrick would sit with Tom and discuss a variety of topics with him. One day, Tom asked Patrick, "Some philosophers and thinkers deny the existence of a conscience within a person. They say that when a person is born, they automatically and gradually acquire knowledge through their senses, such as images and information. As they grow, these things become a guide, law, and conscience within them for the rest of their lives. Is this true?"

Tom replied, "Some philosophers and thinkers have also called for the existence of the conscience's law within a human being. Let's start with an animal, for example. Everyone knows and agrees that what drives an animal is its instincts, which come from its nature. Each animal is distinguished from another by its unique shape and behavior, which are determined by its nature and become its identity. Similarly, a human being has a nature that guides him, and from this, his material personality and identity are formed and exist according to his conscience's law. But there is another factor, the spirit, which also resides within the human being to elevate and distinguish him from other creatures because the soul gives him the ability to think and has the power and control over his conscience and physical desires if it wants."

Patrick asked, "Does instinct guide our conscience since every individual view of conscience is different?"

Tom answered, "If one follows his instincts, they will undoubtedly lead him to peace and freedom since he is a social creature who is at peace with others, and this law lies in his human conscience. But let's not forget that when a person receives information outside of himself through education, regardless of whether it is good or bad, his own thinking stems from his spirit and determines which direction he will take. Animals have a fixed instinct, as we mentioned, but there is another factor that is the most important, and it is the law of the spirit that also resides in man to elevate him and distinguish him from the rest of the creatures because the spirit gives him the ability to think and has the ability and control over the conscience and physical desires if it wants."

*

Tom prepared to travel to spend Christmas with his family; fortunately, the son of Mr. and Mrs. Johnson stayed with his parents. Patrick accompanied Tom to the train station and said goodbye with the hope of meeting again. When the train started heading toward Burbank, Tom's memories began too to float inside and before his eyes. His thoughts and heart ached with sadness for the memories he still had until he arrived.

His whole family, including the kids, welcomed him with open arms. They were so happy to see him, and he was so happy to see them. The next day, Tom bought a Christmas tree, decorated it with black leaves, and built a beautiful grotto at its base. Then, he installed lanterns outside and around the whole house.

Everything around them was inviting joy and happiness, but the hearts of the Aphram family were still sad over the loss of Markus. The day before Christmas, Tom gathered Peter, Amanda, and Lauren and took them to the market to choose their presents. After he bought them gifts, he took them to McDonald's.

The kids were nosy and asked Tom about the cows, chickens, and ducks on the farm. Tom answered them in a funny way to make the holiday more cheerful. The most amazing and valuable times in someone's life are the ones from their childhood because they'll stay with them forever.

It was Christmas Eve, and the entire family was celebrating together; the table was set with the finest foods and beverages. Everyone sat around the table, and the father prayed the

Christmas prayer, as he always did, saying, "On the night of Your birth, O Lord, blessings came, and salvation came to all the peoples of the earth who were under the yoke of slavery and death. With Your coming, You loosened the chains and gave us hope for eternal life. O, Lord! Make us among the chosen ones whose names are written in the book of Your kingdom. Amen."

When they started eating, Amalia said, "I want to share some exciting news with you all on this joyful occasion. Natalie told me she's expecting a baby."

Everyone was overjoyed by the news, and the mother's tears flowed with happiness. She said, "This is the happiest news I've heard in my life."

After they had Christmas dinner, Santa Claus came and gave presents to both the young and the old. It was indescribable how much joy the children felt during this warm holiday, in which they received many presents. At midnight, the church doors were open for the Christmas Mass, so Tom took his parents to the church to share this blessed holiday.

Tom had not yet reconciled with his God but had gone with his parents just to please them. Tom spent New Year's Eve with the family, and during that time, he often visited the places where he and Maria had sat together to recall his memories. After three weeks, Tom said goodbye to his family again and went back to the farm.

Upon his return, he resumed reading and contemplating. His only concern was finding the answers to the question occupying his mind: Why does a good man have to suffer on this earth? Why do evil forces have power over him, and why can they change his future whenever they want? Why does evil sometimes triumph over good? He read books on theology, philosophy, and religion with great interest and understanding, but he was unable to find a solution to his rage. The years passed, one after the other until he spent fourteen years studying books, but to no avail.

One day, he received a call from his brother, Manuel, informing him that their father was very sick and that he needed to see him before it was too late. The call worried Tom, so he informed Mr. Johnson of his sudden departure and prepared for the trip.

Tom's beard was long, but he didn't care how he looked. He could take the train and get to his father's house the same day. He went to his father's room and saw him lying on the bed, seriously ill. He approached his father and sat by his side without finding words to ease his pain.

"I had a beautiful dream about you a while ago, and I have to tell you about it before I die," the father said. He then went on to say, "In the dream, I saw that you became a great doctor who helps many people to get better. My interpretation of this dream, my son, is that you will find the answers to the questions you have been looking for and be able to help other people who are in the same situation as you." Tom grabbed his dad's hand and gave it a kiss.

After that, his father fought death for a few hours until his heart stopped beating all at once, and he died. Tom was filled with tears and regretted leaving the family for all those years instead of staying and providing support. Then, his mother, sister, and brother entered the room and cried with him. The following day, the funeral services took the necessary steps, placed the body in a coffin, and transported it to the church. The family of the deceased had informed relatives and friends to attend the funeral.

In the church, after the priest had completed the prayers and rituals, Tom approached the pulpit to address the mourners. With tears in his eyes, he looked out to the gathering and said: "My father lived his life in fear of the Lord and was steadfast in his devotion to Him. He was a loving husband to my mother and a devoted father to his children.

"When he moved to the city, he got a job in a lumber shop where the owner was mean and stingy. He sometimes asked the workers to work more hours, but he didn't pay them enough for it. But my dad didn't tell him off or quit his job. Instead, he prayed for him, asking the Lord to open his heart and eyes to more important and valuable things in life.

"As time went by, the owner of the lumber shop slowly changed his treatment and began to treat his workers fairly and with respect. One day, the owner called my father into his office and said, 'You really turned my view on life and people around. Your dedication and honesty at work made me feel guilty for how I treated you and everyone else and made me see how wrong I was. Kudos to you, man.'

"Eventually, when the owner fell sick, he put his shop up for sale, and my dad wanted to buy it with all his heart. And that's what happened—the owner gave him a twenty percent discount on the price of the shop because he appreciated his honesty and efforts. That was my father's philosophy in life: work, perseverance, and faith in God. That's exactly what he taught us."

Following the speech, everyone went to the cemetery to bury another loved one under the soil. Maria was among the mourners there, and she approached Amalia and Tom and comforted them. Amalia said to her brother Tom, "Mary's husband died from a painful illness three months ago."

Tom looked at Maria and said sadly, "I'm sorry about your loss."

Amalia told her brother, "Just mourning here isn't enough; we gotta step up and do what we gotta do for her."

Tom looked into Maria's eyes and said, "We'll do what should be done."

Two days later, Amalia drove her car to her parents' house and took Tom to Maria's house. When they arrived, Tom was amazed by the beauty and grandeur of the house that Maria lived in, which was surrounded by green trees and a flower-filled garden. Maria greeted them, welcomed them, and then invited them to sit in the garden because the weather was beautiful and suitable. Afterward, a young, beautiful girl who looked like Maria came and greeted them.

"This is my daughter, Sarah," Maria introduced Amalia and Tom to her as church friends.

"Wow, time flies in this life; your daughter has grown up so fast," Amalia said.

Maria said, "Yeah, time flies by so fast."

Then Sarah took a seat between them.

Tom said calmly, "We have come to see you today, even though we're late, to express our condolences on the death of Mr. Walter."

"We appreciate and thank you for coming, and I know you weren't in town when my husband passed away," Maria said.

"What was the illness that he was suffering from?" Amalia asked.

"Leukemia. He had been undergoing chemotherapy for a long time, but in the last period, his body was unable to handle it, so he passed away," Maria replied.

Due to the discussion about her father, Sarah's eyes reddened with sadness, so she got up and asked for permission to go to her room. When the maid brought the tea and cake, Maria got up and poured tea for Amalia and Tom, then handed them the cake.

"What a beautiful palace you live in, Maria," Amalia

complimented her.

"Possessions don't make a woman's heart happy; there's something more important than that," Maria commented.

While they were talking, time flew by, and Amalia got up.

"Excuse me, but I have to go back home to prepare dinner for my family," Amalia said.

"No problem. I'll ask the driver to take Tom back home," Maria said.

Tom and Maria were silent for a time after Amalia left, but eventually, their emotions and memories began to come flooding back.

"Do you remember the day you said to me that I was your world and that you could not stand a single day without seeing me or hearing my voice?" Maria asked sadly. "Three months ago, my husband died. I knew you heard the news, but I didn't get any messages of sympathy or words of hope that I was still your only love. Have you forgotten me or stopped caring about our love?"

"Maria, this is a complicated situation," Tom said, "but just so you know, my feelings for you are still strong and will never change for life."

"Since the day I got married, my heart has bled every day being away from you," Maria said. "Although I was loyal to my husband and devoted to him, I couldn't get rid of your love in my heart. So why do we torture ourselves in this way? Fate brings us together again, so why should we separate once more? Let's get back together and make the most of what's left because life still has a smile for us. We can still reach the dreams we had when we were younger."

Tom said, "You know how much I love you, right? That's why, after your wedding, I went and isolated myself from the world. My mind is cluttered now, and I need some time to figure things out. I hope you can understand me." After that, the driver took Tom back to his parents' house.

Music was Maria's go-to escape from painful reality whenever she fell into a spiral of sadness. She walked into her room and put down one of Sarah Brightman's records. While listening to the songs, she cried, imagining that Tom had left her and gone back to his farm, and she recalled some of her happiest memories, such as the times she had spent with Tom in cafes and at parties. She also recalled her wedding day, when she was in her white dress and looked back toward the church door to see Tom's arrival to save her. She also reminisced about some of the events in her marriage that made her sad and distracted due to her bad luck in love.

Chapter Six

Tom returned to the farm and entered his house, depressed and mentally exhausted. He lay down on his bed and fell into a deep sleep. He dreamed that he was in a sizable forest, walking barefoot and exhausted, with messy hair, a thick beard, and torn clothes. As he approached a large lake with dark water, he noticed a light from the sky descending onto the ground, and its glowing light spread throughout the area.

When Tom saw this light, he became so scared that he fell on his face. A voice came from the light and said, "Why do you look for answers to your questions in your books, son of the Arameans, when you are far from Me? Don't you realize that you will never find the answers you seek? This is because I have the answers you're looking for, not in your books. I will send you My angel, and he will take you on a journey tomorrow and reveal secrets that the sons of humans have never known. Get down into this shallow lake now to learn something." The light then rose to the sky once again.

Tom got into the water and dove, and after rising, his face and clothing changed, and a light shone on them, making him look like an angel. The lake water transformed into crystal-clear water. Then he woke up.

It was six o'clock in the morning when he got up, and he was still surprised by what he saw in the dream. As he was thinking, an angel of light appeared to him and then hid his light, transforming into a human form and saying, "Do not fear, beloved of God; I am the angel of the Lord. I have come to take you on a journey to reveal some secrets, as the Lord God has requested of me. Everything you will go through and every secret I shall reveal to you are written in the books of heaven. Have your breakfast, and tell Mr. Johnson that you won't be leaving your room today because I will take your spirit."

Tom obeyed the angel and followed his instructions. Then the angel said, "Now lie down on your bed and close your eyes."

The First Genesis

In the blink of an eye, Tom saw himself and the angel standing at the foot of a high mountain on one of the planets, with a vast plain extending to the sea before them. He noticed that the colors of the sky and nature were different from what they were on earth. The sun sent light in beautiful, luminous, transparent colors, and the colors of the land and sea changed from time to time.

"This is the planet chosen by the Creator from the beginning," the angel told him. "He arranged its celestial bodies and named it 'the gorgeous planet' because its soil and water are ideal for creating a magnificent paradise.

"After that, God adjusted the weather, then ordered, 'Let the soil grow grass and flowers of many colors and shapes,' and it did. Grass and flowers of all hues and sizes sprouted from the ground, and they didn't need seeds since they were eternal and never faded. Then the Lord God melted the rocky mountains of this planet, extracting from their elements a substance from which He fashioned gentle and luminous bodies, into which He breathed a breath of His immortal spirit, and we became angels.

"When He began to create us angels, He started with the low ranks and worked his way up to the higher ranks. At the beginning, we were divided into three choirs:

"The first: Seraphim – Cherubim – Thrones.

"The second: Powers – Sultans – Sovereignties.

"The third: Principalities – Archangels – Angels.

"Each of these choirs possesses unique characteristics that differentiate them from one another. The Seraphim are characterized by their ardent love for God, the Cherubim by their wisdom and vast knowledge, and the Dominions by their power and service.

"When God completed His work, He saw that everything He had done was good. He then sat on His throne among us, rejoicing in our company while we were delighted and prostrating ourselves in worshiping His holy and mighty greatness because He created us out of love."

"You say that God made you out of the elements on this planet and then put His Spirit in you, but angels don't have bodies made of matter, so how do you explain this?"

"If your knowledge of worldly matters is still incomplete, how will you know about heavenly matters?" the angel said. "Listen to what I am telling you: every moving system in this universe, whether visible or invisible, is composed of and surrounded by matter, and any moving system that does not consist of and is not surrounded by matter does not exist."

"How?" Tom asked.

The angel revealed, "To simplify things, imagine you have a white sheet of paper in your hand, and you contemplate its substance and composition. You will notice that it has a system within it that keeps its shape and existence; within that system, there is movement. If the movement stops, the system vanishes, and if the system vanishes, the paper vanishes as well. There is no system if there is no movement, no movement if there is no matter."

"Are your spirits, which you received from God, also made of invisible matter?" asked Tom.

The angel replied, "Yes, even the entity and system of the

great, majestic Creator God is also composed and enveloped in eternal, sublime, immortal, unlimited matter, free of all blemishes. The difference is that His system is outside the system of time and space, so time and space cannot contain or reach Him because His elements are immortal and not like the rest of the elements that age. He even transformed the matter of the components of our bodies into immortal matter like our spirits. To simplify the matter for you, I cite what the Apostle Paul said in his letter. The first is to the Corinthians, in which he talks about the believers who transition to eternal life: 'They die in their animal body in order to be resurrected again in a body with an immortal spirit.'

"Did God create you as intelligent spirits only, without senses or instincts, as it was said about you?" Tom asked.

"We have senses, but we do not have instincts because our bodies are spiritual and not earthly like yours," the angel replied. "The senses are what give the mind signals of knowledge about what is happening around it, while instincts give signals to the mind about what the organs of the earthly body need and tend toward. God created most of us in His image and breathed His eternal spirit into us. This is how we got our nature, which gave us love, joy, peace, patience, kindness, goodness, faithfulness, and gentleness. Our minds were born from these virtues and the intellectual energy composed of multiple talents, and we became intelligent beings with free will, independent of our Creator."

"Are your bodies naturally ethereal, transparent cytoplasm, or solid?" Tom asked.

"Our bodies are made of a subtle and transparent cytoplasm, but we have the ability to control its elements and turn it into a solid state according to the desired situation and in various sizes," the angel replied.

"Why can't we see you?" Tom inquired.

"Because we are currently hidden, but we can reveal ourselves when the Lord's will come. And when the spirit leaves your physical bodies, you can see us clearly with the eyes of your spiritual bodies," the angel responded.

"Do angels have the same shapes and sizes as people?" Tom asked.

"Most of us share with humans the same form and size, but there are angels whose sizes are three times larger than theirs. As for the angels who serve the throne, their bodies differ because they have wings due to their service and ranks," the angel replied.

"And how did you live on this planet before a third of you fell, as it is mentioned in the Holy Book?" Tom asked.

"Come, and I will show you the time when we used to live with God," the angel said.

The angel took Tom to a different time, and Tom found himself on the same planet, but this time in a gorgeous field of flowers with nice, calming music flowing within him. He felt love all around him, and from where God's throne was, he saw a light with enchanting colors. Tom was overcome with an indescribable sense of joy and happiness.

"Love and happiness have always been present among us here," the angel explained, "and just as soft flower petals open in the morning to receive the sun, we directed our eyes and hearts in each cycle as our planet rotated around itself to receive the Creator's fatherly look. We used to derive energy from the happiness and joy we felt from His presence among us, and darkness never touched our planet because the Creator had placed two great shining stars facing each other in its sky."

Then, the angel led Tom to great stadiums and arenas, saying, "The Lord God initially requested that we build these stadiums and arenas so that the angels could compete in the talents and abilities they possess. After we built them, the competitions began, and the angels gathered on the stadium stands, excited for each skill or talent they competed for and excelled in on the fields and stadiums. To give you a closer idea of the types of games we played, they were similar to the ones you also play in the Olympics, but with greater and grander abilities."

Then the angel showed Tom those amazing games.

The angel added, "Sometimes these competitions would move to outer space in plain view of the angels sitting on the stands, and before them was a visible screen showing what was happening in these competitions. God supervised all these competitions and rewarded the winners, led by the Cherub Lucifer, who always won because he was the most skillful and powerful in terms of talents and abilities. He once competed against other angels to blow up an entire planet, and no one else could do it except him.

"He flew up and penetrated the planet's core like lightning, then used his great power to explode it and turn it into small debris scattered in the vast space. The angels cheered for him at that moment, and his greatness was even more magnified in their eyes. As arrogance and pride because of his glory and power grew in Lucifer's mind, he didn't reject or fight against them. Over time, these two sins turned into rebellion, which turned into disobedience, which turned into a challenge to the Creator and a race for the throne.

"After that, Lucifer gathered with the leaders of the angels before the battle, and present at the meeting were Michael, Gabriel, Raphael, Uriel, Ananiel, Sariel, Suriel, Sadakiel, Ramiel, Malail, Nariel, Adanarel, Yashiel, Ilumael, Shamikha,

Yeqon, Hashbiel, Jedarraiel, Fanuel, Kasdaye, Artaqifa, Kokabiel, Touriel, Daniel, Barquiel, Armros, Petriel, Armen, Basasael, Hananiel, Simapesiel, Yatreiel, Tumiel, and Turial. And there were many leaders who did not attend because they learned of Lucifer's rebellious intentions.

"Lucifer stood among them and said, 'I will no longer accept to submit to the Creator God and obey Him. It is time for me to become independent and become a god-like Him or even greater than Him. I will free everyone who follows me and make him a god, so those who support me can stay, and those who oppose me can leave.'

"Michael stood up against him and told him, 'You are making a grave mistake, and you and all those who will follow you will pay dearly for it.' Then he left the meeting, and so did Gabriel, Raphael, Ananiel, Saratiel, Suriel, Sedakiel, Uriel, Ramiel, Malayal, Narel, Adanarel, Jesuel, and Elumael. From then on, Lucifer, whose name means 'morning planet,' was called 'Satanael,' which means 'God resister.'

"All the forces of the heavens met on the battlefield for the battle. They were split into two groups, one loyal to God the Creator and the other loyal to Satanael because they saw him as their greatest leader. In the days leading up to the battle, God addressed His word to Satanael's followers to retract their decision so that they would not lose their ranks and the glory they were in.

"However, Satanael's strength and delusion blinded them to the truth. As a result, they fought with flaming swords. Satanael engaged in a fierce battle with the leader of the angels, Michael, which Satanael would have won if it hadn't been for the intervention of God, the Creator, who supported Michael and helped him win.

"Following Satanael's defeat, all of his forces fell down, and they lost their bliss. God lost a third of his children as a result of the battle, causing great sadness and anguish in the sky. The world of angels was plunged into this darkness and grief for many aeons after that."

Chapter Seven

The angel took Tom to a different time and dimension and placed him before the throne of God long after a section of the angels had fallen.

Tom kneeled before the throne while the angel revealed to him the archives of the books of the heavens. A strong feeling of sadness emanated from the throne and permeated the surroundings, affecting even Tom. Suddenly, a powerful and bright light emerged from the throne, branching out into three colors: white, red, and yellow. Above the throne, Seraphim fluttered and sang mournful hymns that caused Tom's heart to break with grief.

"Why does the light inside the throne shine in three different colors?" Tom asked the angel this question that suddenly popped into his head.

The angel replied, "Because the three colors symbolize the entity of God, which is a Trinity. The white color symbolizes inner consciousness, the red color symbolizes the mind, and the yellow color symbolizes the spirit. The three have one nature, one essence, and one will, but with three hypostases united without mixing, distinct without division."

"The Trinity has always been a mystery to me. Can you explain it in more detail?" Tom asked.

The angel explained, "The one nature of God is characterized by three properties, that is, by three laws: God's inner consciousness has a law, His divine mind has a law, and His divine spirit has a law. Meaning that within God's being, there is a home for inner consciousness, a home for the mind, and a home for life."

"Why did Jesus Christ use the term 'Father and Son' instead of inner consciousness and mind?" Tom asked.

"Because from the beginning, the hypostasis of the mind was born of the hypostasis of inner consciousness, so Christ used these two terms, Father and Son, to denote birth and the one nature. The first hypostasis, in relation to the second hypostasis, is 'His Father,' but for us as angels and for you as humans, it is the hypostasis of inner consciousness because we are not of its nature and essence like the second hypostasis. The hypostasis of the Holy Spirit also emerged from the hypostasis of inner consciousness. I can give you the metaphor of fire from which light is born, and heat emanates so you can get an idea of the Divine Trinity. The fire represents the Divine inner consciousness, the light of fire represents the Divine mind, and the heat of the fire represents the spirit of the Divine," the angel replied.

After answering all of Tom's questions, the angel added, "Now a dialog between the three hypostases will take place on the throne, and the Lord wants you to listen carefully and write it down. The Holy Trinity has never stopped grieving for what has happened to some of the angels since their fall."

During this divine dialog, Tom tried to listen very carefully.

The hypostasis of the inner consciousness said to the hypostasis of the mind and the hypostasis of the spirit, "I am grieving for Our children whom We have lost. Their cries come up to Us every time because some of them have regretted their actions."

"Satan deceived them, so they fell," said the hypostasis of

the mind.

The hypostasis of the Spirit also added, "Although, they were not lacking in knowledge, the majority of them fell because they were unable to distinguish truth from falsehood in the situation that Satan had placed them in. They lacked the necessary experience to differentiate between good and evil."

The hypostasis of mind then stated, "This experience can only be obtained when the spirit wears a heavy material form."

"I am willing to set up a system for those who have repented that provides them with everything they need to wear the heavy material, experience and learn, and then return to Us," the hypostasis of the inner consciousness suggested.

"I am also willing to wear the heavy material like them to guide them, teach them, and pay the price for the sin they committed against Us," the hypostasis of the mind added.

Then, the hypostasis of the Spirit also spoke and said, "I will pour out My Spirit within them so that they may walk in the paths of love, truth, and righteousness."

At this time, the angels of the heavens blew their trumpets, announcing the good news that would be recited to them by their God. Everyone rejoiced, and joy filled the air, and the sky's bright colors came back. The angels gathered around the throne. They bowed down and looked up at their Creator, waiting for Him to speak.

Then a great and majestic voice came from the throne, saying, "My beloved children, I want you to rejoice with Me because I have decided to build a new solar system, the goal of which is to pave the way and qualify your brothers who fell with Satan for the kingdom again because some of them regretted what they did. I consider it fair to give them another chance to return to Us if they successfully pass the tests and experiments while wearing the heavy-material garment. And you also have a role in this work for the salvation of your repentant brethren."

The angels of all ranks bowed before the throne, saying in unison, "Glory, power, and praise be to You, and praise forever and ever, for You are the God of wisdom, justice, and mercy."

God commanded the angels to get ready to descend to the planet of the abyss with the second hypostasis to preach salvation to the repentant. In the blink of an eye, the angelic ships were ready for the mission. Afterward, all the ships headed toward the planet of the abyss, with the Lord guiding them, and Tom was watching all these events with the angel.

When the Lord's ship touched down on the planet of the abyss, the whole place shook. The surface of the abyss was barren, with many mountains and dark caves where countless souls lived, and from that place emanated foul odors. The fallen angels attempted to approach the Lord's ship, believing that their Creator was in it, prostrating themselves and seeking salvation from Him. When the Lord appeared before the fallen angels, He lit up the place with His light. He then spoke to them, saying, "I'm here to tell you that those who repented of their disobedience and stayed in truth and love will be saved from punishment and put back where they were before."

All the remorseful angels were filled with joy because hope emerged for their salvation. Then Satan showed up among them, scary and ugly. He had two big eyes that showed hatred and anger, two long ears like wolves', and two black horns that stuck out from the top of his head. He spoke to the second hypostasis and said, "These souls are mine, and no one can take them from me."

The Lord said to him, "Some of them are no longer loyal to you because they regretted what they had done, so since I am their creator, I have the right to them as well. I will test each one of them, and you will have the right to try them as well, according to the capacity of each spirit. Whoever passes the test will be Mine, and whoever fails will go back to you."

"However, there is a price to pay," Satan replied.

"I will pay for their sins," said the Lord.

"But I don't want or need all this bargaining," Satan replied.

"Not as you want, but as the truth wants," The Lord said.

Angered, Satan attempted to attack the Lord, but the Lord released a powerful energy that thundered and terrified Satan and his followers.

This was what happened before God began creating the world, and the purpose of all of this was for these angels to take on earthly bodies through birth in order to learn about and experience good and evil. Through that heavy material, they would choose one of two paths: either the path of good, which was the path of truth leading to bliss, or the path of evil, which was falsehood leading to perdition.

The Second Genesis

After that, the angel took Tom to space and showed him how God arranged the celestial bodies and formed the solar system, placing the Earth in one of its orbits and bestowing upon it a moon, which orbits around it and shines light on its dark side along with the stars.

Then the angel said, "God created a firmament in the center of the waters to separate them, and God named the firmament the 'sky.' Then, God gathered the waters under the sky into a single place, and dry ground appeared; God named the dry ground 'land' and the gathered waters 'seas.' God commanded, 'Let the earth bring forth vegetation: plants yielding seed, and fruit trees bearing fruit in which is their seed, each according to its kind.' And the earth brought forth vegetation: plants yielding seed according to their own kinds, and trees bearing fruit in which is their seed, each according to its kind. Then God said, 'Let the waters teem with living fish and reptiles and let the earth bear living creatures of their kind.'

"And after all this, God created man from the dust of the ground and breathed into his nostrils the breath of life. Adam became a living being in the image of God, like His example. Then, from Adam's rib, He created Eve, and the Lord God planted a garden in Eden, in the east, and sent Adam and Eve there and commanded them, 'Eat from all the trees of the garden, but from the tree of the knowledge of good and evil, you will die on the day you eat it.' God saw that everything He made was good. And on the seventh day, God rested from all His work, as recorded in the Book of Genesis.

"Satan entered the Garden of Eden disguised as a serpent and asked Eve, 'Did God really say, "You must not eat from any tree in the garden?"'

"The woman said to the serpent, 'We may eat fruit from the trees in the garden, but God did say, "You must not eat fruit from the tree that is in the middle of the garden, and you must not touch it, or you will die."'

"'You will not certainly die,' the serpent said to the woman. 'For God knows that when you eat from it, your eyes will be opened, and you will be like God, knowing good and evil.'

"The woman saw that the fruit of the tree was good for food and pleasing to the eye. So, she took some and ate it, and she also gave some to her husband, who was with her, and he ate it. Then, both of them opened their eyes, and they realized they were naked, so they made aprons out of fig leaves. When the day's wind blew, they heard the Lord God's footsteps in the garden, so they hid among the trees from the sight of the Lord God.

"But the Lord God called to the man, 'Where are you?'

"Adam replied, 'I heard Your voice, and I was afraid because I was naked, so I hid.'

"Then the Lord God asked, 'Who told you that you were naked? Have you eaten from the tree that I commanded you not to eat from?'

"Adam answered, 'The woman you put here with me gave me some fruit from the tree, and I ate it.'

"Then the Lord God said to the woman, 'What is this you have done?'

"The woman said, 'The serpent deceived me, and I ate.'

"So, the Lord God said to the serpent, 'Because you have

done this, cursed are you above all livestock and all wild animals! You will crawl on your belly, and you will eat dust all the days of your life. And I will put enmity between you and the woman and between your offspring and hers; they will crush your head, and you will strike their heels.'

"Then he said to the woman, 'I will overburden you so that you will give birth to children in pain and long for your husband, and he will rule over you.'

"Then to Adam, He said, 'Because you have heeded the voice of your wife and have eaten from the tree from which I commanded you not to eat, the earth is cursed because of you. In toil, you shall eat of it all the days of your life. Both thorns and thistles shall grow for you, and you shall eat the grass of the field. In the sweat of your brow, you shall eat bread until you return to the ground from which you were taken; for dust you are, and to dust you shall return.'"

The angel said to Tom, "The sin committed by Adam and Eve symbolizes the sin of the fallen angels. As you can see, both of them (humans and angels) disobeyed the Lord God's commandments and wanted to become gods. Both of them were also lured into temptation by Satan. The purpose of the Adam and Eve story and their fall is that God wanted to show man that he is incomplete, imperfect, and has limited experience, so he always makes mistakes, but to become righteous, one must learn from life experience, cling to virtues, and follow God's commandments, which contain life and truth.

"God allowed fallen angels to come through Adam's lineage while keeping this secret hidden from them. Those who follow God's will shall attain salvation, while those who follow the path of evil shall return to the abyss. These are the secrets that God wanted you to understand because you have spent part of your life questioning them. Finally, before you appear before the Lord, I'd like to take you to visit the soul of your brother Marcus in the highest paradise, where saints and the pious live."

In a flash, Tom and the angel were standing on a vast green plain, the road before them paved with light sapphire stones and flanked by vibrant flowers. As they drew closer to the dwellings of the saints, Tom felt a sense of inner calm and comfort, and then he saw a group of righteous people wearing bright white clothing that emitted light. When Tom saw his father and his brother Marcus among the righteous, he ran up to them, hugged them, and cried with joy at seeing them again. "Me, Mom, Amalia, and Manuel all missed you," Tom exclaimed with joy at his brother.

Marcus also expressed his longing for them, stating, "There will come a day when all of us will meet again and live together, and death will not separate us after that." Tom's father then introduced him to his grandparents, who were also present, and Tom was happy to meet them.

After that, the angel took Tom again and carried him to another dimension, where he found himself in front of God's throne, and a bright light filled the place with its three colors: white, red, and yellow. Tom fell to his knees and bowed his head in awe of the greatness and majesty of the place. He felt a deep sense of being in the presence of his Creator, the source of his life. The Seraphim fluttered around the throne, singing sweet and enchanting hymns of joy. Then, the light came out of the throne and transformed into a quasi-human form. He approached him and said to him in a warm and affectionate voice, "Raise your head, Tom."

When Tom raised his head, he found himself in the presence of his Lord and God, Jesus Christ. His face resembled the artists' paintings, but His appearance was even more beautiful and glorious here, as a great light shone from His face and clothes.

Tom said, "Forgive me, Lord, for my rebellion and lack of faith."

Christ answered, "You have been dear and precious to Us, Tom, and because you have walked uprightly throughout your life, We have given you this gift, which is the knowledge of what happened in the first and second Genesis. The time has come for the churches to know what happened during that time. I want you to record everything you saw and heard and send it to the churches."

After that, the Lord asked him, as he asked Peter, "Do you love me, Tom?"

Tom answered, "Yes, Lord, I am ready to give my life for You, if necessary, now that I have understood the truth."

Christ said to him, "Satan will not let you rest, so hold fast to your faith and your love of goodness." Then the Lord blessed him and said, "Go in peace."

Chapter Eight

After coming home from his visit with the angel at midnight, Tom was startled when his spirit returned to him. Tom then kneeled down, lifted his head to the sky, and prayed, "O Lord of the universe and creator of angels and humans through love, forgive my frailties and mistakes; You are the Almighty over everything. My Creator, make me an obedient instrument in Your hands so that I can walk on Your path until the end of my days."

After Tom finished his prayer, he sat down and began to write down everything he had seen and heard in heaven.

At seven in the morning, Tom went to work, and Mr. Johnson followed him as well. At lunchtime, Tom told Mr. and Mrs. Johnson what had happened to him the previous night and how the angel had taken his spirit and raised it to heaven, revealing many secrets to him.

After telling them his story, he said, "Now we gotta find someone to work on the farm 'cause I'm gonna head back to the city. I've got stuff to do there, and there's also a bride waiting for me."

The farmer and his wife were happy to hear this good news, and they wished him luck and happiness in his life. Within a few days, Mr. Johnson was able to hire another worker from a nearby area. Thus, Tom bid Mr. and Mrs. Johnson farewell, promising to visit them once a year.

Tom returned to his parents' home, overwhelmed with happiness. He told his mother what had happened to him and called Maria to let her know he wanted to see her at the coffee shop where they used to meet. In about thirty minutes, the two of them sat down with joy and longing in their eyes.

Tom shared with her all that he had experienced and heard in heaven and said, "Now, honey, we can marry and make our dreams come true, but let's wait for some time to show respect for your husband's and my dad's passing."

Maria got up and gave him a hug. Tears of happiness ran down her face. In the evening, the family gathered at their parents' home, and Tom told them about the dream he had seen in heaven, especially when he met Marcus and his father. Tears of joy streamed down their faces.

The next day, Tom brought the letters in which he had written down all the secrets related to his dream and sent them to the three churches: the Orthodox, the Catholics, and the mother, the Lutheran Church.

That night, the devil dispatched two servants to steal Tom's spirit so that he would appear before him in the abyss. When they brought him, the devil gave him a mean look and said, "Welcome, brave commander 'Armaros.' Was it easy to turn against your master, to whom you swore allegiance on the day of the battle?"

Tom said, "You tricked me and a lot of other angels by leading them astray."

Satan said to him, "Listen if you do what I order you to do, I will let you marry your beloved and live a life of luxury. But if you refuse to comply, I will make you paralyzed and incapable of doing anything."

Tom replied, "I will no longer follow your orders. Because of you, the spirits of angels in heaven and on earth have suffered. You have control over my body but not over my spirit, so do whatever you want." The devil grew enraged and yelled, "Take him away from me!"

When Tom's spirit was given back to him by Satan's servants, he felt a great deal of pain in his back. He asked his mother to call an ambulance to take him to the hospital. In the meantime, his mother called his brother and sister to catch them up on the news. After the tests, it was found that Tom had a spinal cord injury, and the condition he was suffering from was lower paraplegia. He became unable to move the lower half of his body.

The next day, Maria heard the news and rushed to visit him in the hospital. She sat beside him, held his hand, and hugged him while tears streamed down her eyes. Tom said to her, "We ain't gonna chase our dreams no more 'cause I'm helpless now."

She said, shedding tears, "This illness won't keep us apart."

Tom wiped away her tears and said to her, "This is not the right time to talk about this matter."

After the doctors finished the tests, Tom was transferred to his parents' house in a wheelchair. After six months, Maria convinced Tom to marry her, and when he agreed, she asked the wedding planner to set up her garden for the wedding.

On the wedding day, the weather was beautiful, and the sky was clear blue. The invitees, headed by the priest, showed up, and the garden was brimming with roses and adorned with beautiful, colorful decorations.

At the appointed time, the bride and her groom, Tom, who was in a wheelchair, made their way to the priest. The priest started the wedding prayer and eventually reached the part where the bride and groom were asked.

The priest asked Tom, "Do you want Maria to be your wife?"

Tom answered, "Yes."

Then the priest asked Maria, "Do you want Tom to be your

husband?"

She replied, "Yes."

Immediately, the women cheered and shouted. As soon as the priest finished the wedding ceremony and the newlyweds kissed each other, the music started to play. Suddenly, the same angel appeared to Tom and said to him, "Since you revealed the secrets of the angels to the churches of Christ, the angels of heaven loved you, and they pleaded before the Lord God to heal you and reward you on the day of your wedding, and here He has granted their prayers."

The angel told Tom to look up at the sky, and when he did, he couldn't believe what he saw. The angels were watching the wedding, and the sky was filled with their most beautiful, colorful decorations.

Tom asked the angel to let Maria see what he saw, and the angel said that God had granted his wish. Then he disappeared.

Tom called out to Maria, and she approached him. Then he said to her, "Look up at the sky." She almost fainted after looking up at the sky.

Tom said to her, "Give me your hand and help me stand up and dance with you."

But she didn't believe what she heard from her groom. She took his hand and helped him stand up, and then he hugged her with joy. They danced, and the sky began to rain with small, colorful leaves that were tinted with the colors of the rainbow. The guests were amazed by what they saw.

To Dear Readers

Dear Friends, I'd like to let you know that the events in this story are entirely made up by my imagination. I created its events and scenes to express my philosophical and theological thoughts and deciphered its symbols to make its dimensions and concepts easily accessible. At the same time, these ideas did not appear out of nowhere, but they were the product of careful contemplation and deduction, and they were based on the Holy Bible. I hope you continue reading so you can discover how I arrived at presenting the two most important theories in this book, namely the theory of the *Modern Holy Trinity Secret* and the theory of the *Fallen Angels Secret*.

Explanation of the Two Theories

I think that whoever reads this short novel has gotten an idea of the two modern theories related to the mystery of the Holy Trinity and the fallen angels, which I presented in the book indirectly. It is certain that some questions will arise in your thoughts about them. Therefore, I wanted to shed light and delve into some of the facts and secrets of these two theories so that you can understand my vision and how I arrived at these conclusions. First, my intention in all of this is for us to have a clear picture of this Almighty, loving, living God who exists in heaven so that our relationship with Him becomes more solidified from a practical and cognitive standpoint. At the same time, this information is a service to future generations. Second, I shed light on the fallen angels, who, according to my belief, have a relationship and role in our human lives. Since these two main ideas about the mystery of the Holy Trinity and the fallen angels have become like theories, I must explain them with evidence and proof.

I want you to know that I did not come up with the theory of fallen angels out of nowhere or from imagination, but rather I deduced this from verses found in the Old and New Testaments of the Bible, which indicate that the theory may be almost correct, even if it is not mentioned in the Bible explicitly. Before I begin the explanation, I would also like to say that everything that I will mention and cite related to these two issues is considered theological and philosophical thoughts. Regardless of whether we believe in these two propositions or not, it will not affect the essence of our faith because it does not affect the 'Law of Faith,' which is the constitution of our Orthodox, Catholic, and Lutheran churches (the Protestant Mother Church). To clarify, with regard to the mystery of the Holy Trinity in this book, I do not diminish the value of the Father, the Son, or the Holy Spirit, as Arius and Nestorius did. Rather, I believe that the Father, the Son, and the Holy Spirit are one God in three persons of equal essence, as the Holy Universal Church believes.

The Modern Theory Related to the Secret of the Holy Trinity (Part One)

For definition: I mentioned at the beginning of the book, and I will also mention here that I will use two important terms in the book. The first is 'hypostasis,' which means 'an entity that shares nature and essence with another entity and is united with it in one being or in one body, regardless of whether it is spiritual or material, and each of these two or more hypostases has free will and a characteristic that differs from the other.'

The second term is 'inner consciousness,' which, according to my view and belief, has an entity and free will, whether it is within God or within man. Within this entity, there is a law of high morals and noble feelings. Whenever I mention the term 'inner consciousness' in the book, remember that I mean it in this sense.

I will now put here, before I begin, the dialog that took place between Tom and the angel regarding the first theory, *The Secret of the Holy Trinity*, just as a reminder, and then I will begin the explanation using evidence.

"Why does the light inside the throne shine in three different colors?" Tom asked the angel this question that suddenly popped into his head.

The angel replied, "Because the three colors symbolize the entity of God, which is a Trinity. The white color symbolizes inner consciousness, the red color symbolizes the mind, and the yellow color symbolizes the spirit. The three have one nature, one essence, and one will, but with three hypostases united without mixing, distinct without division."

"The Trinity has always been a mystery to me. Can you explain it in more detail?" Tom asked.

The angel explained, "The one nature of God is characterized by three properties, that is, by three laws: God's inner consciousness has a law, His divine mind has a law, and His divine spirit has a law. Meaning that within God's being, there is a home for consciousness, a home for the mind, and a home for life."

"Why did Jesus Christ use the term 'Father and Son' instead of consciousness and mind?" Tom asked.

"Because from the beginning, the hypostasis of the mind was born of the hypostasis of the inner consciousness, so Christ used these two terms, Father and Son, to denote birth and the one nature. The first hypostasis, in relation to the second hypostasis, is 'His Father,' but for us as angels and for you as humans, it is the hypostasis of inner consciousness because we are not of its nature and essence like the second hypostasis. The hypostasis of the Holy Spirit also emerged from the hypostasis of inner consciousness. I can give you the metaphor of fire from which light is born and heat emanates, so you can get an idea of the Divine Trinity. The fire represents the Divine inner consciousness, the light of fire represents the Divine mind, and the heat of the fire represents the spirit of the Divine," the angel replied.

Now we return to the explanation: Since we are in the image and likeness of God, as stated in the Book of Genesis, this means that there is a similarity between us and God, both formally and internally. But the difference between us is that God is unlimited, and we are limited. His nature is perfect, and our nature as human beings is weak and imperfect. In order for us to be able to understand the secret of the Holy Trinity and give a clear picture of it, we must first understand the nature of man because through it, we will hold the thread that leads us to understand the secret of the nature of God, which is a Trinity, and this research will give us clearer ideas about it. I will first begin by explaining the mind, and then the spirit's turn will come.

I will now seek the help of some scientists and doctors in the field of the human brain and see what they said and wrote about it: "The human brain consists of three main sections. The first section is called the brainstem, and it is responsible for all the functions of the human body, such as breathing, the heartbeat system, the senses, instincts, etc. The second section is called the limbic system, and it is responsible for emotions, such as adherence to values and morals, respect, compassion, etc. Then the third section is called the cerebral cortex, and it is responsible for knowledge, logic, imagination, language, etc."

Let's now return to the brain stem. This section has several branches. Animals also have only this section of the brain. As a result, we can see that humans and animals share common denominators such as senses, instincts, and emotions like fear, anger, joy, and sadness. The same can be said for meekness, intimacy, loyalty, and a variety of other characteristics. These unique qualities found in animals, however, are not due to free will but rather due to instincts that God has implanted in them, giving each animal an advantage.

The second part of the brain (known as the limbic system) is responsible for 'ideal' and 'noble' feelings, such as adherence to values and morals, generosity, worship, feelings of guilt, compassion, ideal and not instinctive love, friendship, respect, etc.

Have you ever asked yourselves how this part of the mind gets its information?

Perhaps some of you will respond, "From good educational teachings which are passed down from one generation to another." After getting this answer, I will ask you again: Where did the parents or teachers get these sublime teachings?

Some of you will answer, "They got it from thinkers and philosophers throughout the ages."

After the second answer, I will ask a third question. Where did thinkers and philosophers get this information from? Some will answer, "Thinkers and philosophers deduced this information from thought." The answer is correct, meaning that they deduced this information about ethics and ideals from the limbic system and not from people's experience because life cannot teach people things that they do not possess, such as ethics and ideals, if they are not present in human thought from the beginning.

In the same vein, Plato says, "Everything in this life is a representation of the afterlife." Meaning that the original copy is not in this life but rather in the afterlife, and we as humans derive all knowledge that is above matter from the afterlife.

After this explanation, a question that imposes itself on us will immediately come to mind: Where does the limbic system derive its information?

As we mentioned, the brainstem derives its information from the soul, which is affiliated with the body's organs and is nourished by it. However, the limbic system derives its information from the inner consciousness because, within the inner consciousness, there is the law of the noble and ideal human feelings. We do not find these feelings in animals. Although they have a brain like a human, they lack these feelings because, as we mentioned, they do not have a limbic system (i.e., inner consciousness), and they also do not have a cerebral cortex. Therefore, they do not enjoy thought but are guided by the rule of their instincts, nothing more.

The third section of the brain (the cerebral cortex) also contains a law, which is responsible, as I mentioned before, for knowledge, logic, imagination, language, etc. Here, I would like to repeat and say that human beings will not be able to recognize and reach sublime knowledge and ideals if there are no much higher entities than matter that are revealed to them.

In adulthood, a person's abilities reach a state of maturity, and we can group them into three systems: a system that contains mental ability (Mind), a system that contains emotional ability (Inner consciousness), and a system that contains both physical and psychological ability (Soul).

The mental ability contains the law of thought through which a person can enact laws and regulations. Thought is also characterized by faculties, from which knowledge and talents of all kinds are generated. As for inner consciousness, man has another law that differs from the law of thought. From it, a person derives good behaviors that are related to noble and ideal human feelings, such as non-instinctive love, compassion, charity, devotion to others, etc.

In the section of the mind, which is concerned with the brainstem, there is the physical and psychological ability of a person, and there is also an innate human law related to the body. From it, a person can deduce his way of living and distinguish what is good or evil for him in this life. This innate physical law gives man his correct identity, as is the case with other animals from a physical perspective. It is the one that provides the human thinking mind and the emotional mind with theoretical and emotional information related to instincts, and it tries to preserve their existence through its desires and appetites.

We cannot mix these systems because when we think, we do not feel any sense of the thought or even the idea that we are thinking about. In addition, when we feel, the mind does not find any thoughts within these feelings because each language system differs from the other. As for the soul system, which is subordinate to the body, it is lower in rank than these two systems because of its controlling system that lacks free will.

This means that within a person, there are two active forces with free will: a purely mental force and a purely inner consciousness force, and each of them has a free will that is independent of the other. Since the ability of the mind has a property and the ability of the inner consciousness has a property, we conclude that within the human body, there are two hypostasis: the hypostasis of the mind and the hypostasis of the inner consciousness.

As I mentioned, the system of the soul is subordinate to the physical body; it is governed. Therefore, we cannot give it the title of hypostasis, even though it shares its system with the mind and inner consciousness systems in the same body.

Now, I'd like to give some examples that show that both the mind and the inner consciousness have free will.

In general, we notice that the mind has the authority to make most decisions freely, as it is qualified and prepared for this task. It is, for example, responsible for enacting laws and enforcing justice and peace in societies, which does not necessitate evidence or proof.

As for the freedom of inner consciousness, I will give two

real examples that occurred in history. The first was in 1936, when Prince Edward VIII ascended the throne and became King of England following his father's death. At that time, he loved Mrs. Wallis Simpson and wanted to marry her, but she was divorced. The royal family and some influential figures in the state refused this because it would bring shame to the kingdom.

They gave the king a choice between the throne and the divorced woman. He chose the woman. He loved and abdicated the throne of his own free will. Here, we notice that if King Edward had listened to the voice of reason and submitted to it, he could have ruled the empire for a long time and married the most beautiful girl in England. However, the feelings in his inner consciousness prevailed, and they made the decision freely. This king chose the woman he loved instead of the throne and glory. There is a second example in Emperor Antony, who loved Queen Cleopatra and could not bear to leave her. When the Roman soldiers asked him to return to Rome and sit on the throne and rule his people, he refused, which led to a war in which his love for Cleopatra cost him his life. There are many examples like these if we search in books and examine history carefully.

Here, I want to give a very important piece of information: Most girls and women are subject to their inner consciousness more than their minds because inner consciousness is where feelings emerge. Is this wrong, or right? In my opinion, it depends on the situation. The majority of men believe that this choice is wrong because they are more rational than women, but the majority of girls and women believe that this choice is the correct one for them. It is because, in it, they feel alive and find a meaning for their existence.

A Modern Theory About the Secret of the Holy Trinity (Part Two)

Now, it's time for the spirit. Since we believe in God and spirits, we must trust and believe what the Bible says about man. For this reason, I'm going to cite a few verses in order to gradually show you how the link between the human spirit and the physical brain is established.

I will start with the first verse, which is from Genesis 2:7: "Then the Lord God formed the man of dust from the ground and breathed into his nostrils the breath of life, and the man became a living creature."

In this verse, we notice that God gave man the breath of life (the spirit), which brought him to life. Some of you may say that animals also live on this earth, even though God did not give them the breath of life. I agree with you that the same animal was taken from the earth and will return to it. However, humans have been distinguished by their soul and spirit. The human soul is also perishable (its body) because it was taken from the dust, but its spirit is eternal.

Why?

Because God created us from His holy spirit through this breath that He breathed into Adam. The proof of this is found in Mark 12:27, when Christ spoke with the Jews and said, "He is not the

God of the dead, but the God of the living. You are badly mistaken!"

This shows that God is not the God of the dead but of the living. My question to you now is this: Is the spirit within us just an energy that gives us life, or does it have other characteristics?

The answer to this question can be found in 1 Corinthians 2:11, where the apostle Paul says, "For who knows a person's thoughts except their own spirit within them?"

Here, Paul attributes the power of thought to the spirit within a person. Also, in Paul's letter to Galatians 5:22, he says, "But the fruit of the Spirit is love, joy, peace, forbearance, kindness, goodness, faithfulness."

We see that the spirit is not only associated with thought but also with feelings. I will also cite the final verse, the first letter of Peter 4:10, which says: "Each of you should use whatever gift you have received to serve others, as faithful stewards of God's grace in its various forms."

The word 'gift' here means ability or skill. As we saw in the verse, God distributed these gifts to the spirits of believers to meet the needs of the church, such as preaching, healing, speaking in the tongues of the prophets, etc. All these gifts are attributed to the spirit and not to the human brain. What is remarkable is that the spirit did not acquire thought, virtues, and talents from the human brain; rather, the opposite is true, as the brain acquired and enriched itself from the richness of the spirit.

Why?

Because of all the spiritual knowledge, equations, systems, and even feelings that emanate from inner consciousness, if their original copy was not present in the human spirit, the brain, with its two parts, the limbic system and its cortex, would not be aware of and realize those noble feelings and equations.

For example, if we put a lamb or another type of animal in a university classroom, how will it understand what the professor is saying if it lacks the faculties of thought and powers? What I mean is that if the spirit did not exist within humans, they would be very similar to animals. Therefore, the credit belongs not to the human brain (soul) but to the spirit, in which the laws and systems related to thought and noble feelings lie.

However, the material (the physical brain) aids the spirit in discovering the knowledge contained within it, and the physical brain also aids the spirit in gaining experience through the life experiences it has had in this physical body on earth. The spirit discovers its flaws and mistakes while also learning from its experiences and taking a stand on the issues it tests, such as good and evil, truth from falsehood, and right from wrong. The evidence for what I'm saying can be found in the Gospel of Matthew 5:1–12, specifically in the Sermon on the Mount and the Beatitudes. If we contemplate what Christ said in these verses, we can summarize them in one sentence: "Blessed are those who endure these trials and remain righteous."

Gifts and even moral virtues do not exist in the material human brain but rather come from the spirit, which feeds the brain with skills in the same way that the brain feeds on the body's senses and emotions. I think the picture is clear now: The human brainstem can guide and maintain the physical body. From the limbic system, humans derive their moral feelings, and from the cerebral cortex, they derive their ideas. These two sections (the limbic system and the cerebral cortex) are almost united by the living spirit.

The spirit has two free will hypostases: the intellect and the inner consciousness, which God has bestowed upon us. From this, we can infer and have a clear idea of the mystery of the Holy Trinity. When Christ came to Earth, he declared that God is a Trinity. Therefore, we see that the fathers of the Church preserved this idea and affirmed that God has three properties and provided examples to prove it; one of the most famous examples is the sun. They claimed that the sun has three properties: the entity of the sun, which represents the entity of God; the light that it emits, which represents the intellect; and the heat that it emits, which represents the spirit.

We can present the same example in another way: The sun in the sky represents the Father, the light among us represents the Son, and the warmth that penetrates within us represents the Holy Spirit.

However, there has always been a missing and ambiguous link in the mystery of the Holy Trinity: If the Son is the hypostasis of the mind as mentioned in the Bible, then what is the role and function of the hypostasis of the Father? As for the hypostasis of the Holy Spirit, as we know, it is the life-giving spirit. Therefore, after deep contemplation and thought for a period of time, a theological idea, or rather a thought, came to my mind to decipher the symbols of this mystery: If the Son is the mind, which is the Word as mentioned in the first chapter of the Gospel of John, then the Father would be the inner consciousness, and here I will give some examples that confirm and validate this belief.

I will start with the first piece of evidence, which is 'like the sun,' which I mentioned a little while ago, but I will present it in a different way and view: The sun contains billions of volcanoes within it. If we say, for example, that the Father symbolizes the entity of the sun, the energy it contains is similar to inner consciousness because, in inner consciousness, there is also energy within which billions of feelings and systems mix. The light of the sun symbolizes the mind, which reflects what is inside the sun. The heat of the sun symbolizes the Holy Spirit, meaning life. I do not think that we are mistaken if we believe that the Father is the inner consciousness, the Son is the mind, and the Holy Spirit is the life-giving spirit.

As for the second evidence, it is found in 1 John 4:8, when he says, "Whoever does not love does not know God, because God is love." In this verse, we see that there is a great place for feelings inside His inner consciousness, as well as a place for the mind and a place for life, namely the Holy Spirit. I wonder: Why haven't the Church Fathers and even theologians recognized and admitted that there is a hypostasis inside God called the inner consciousness, from which virtues and noble emotions flow?

The third evidence is in Matthew 11:29, where Jesus says, "Take My yoke upon you and learn from Me, for I am gentle and humble in heart, and you will find rest for your souls." Of course, Jesus here did not mean the physical heart, which is an organ that pumps blood, but rather that he has a heart filled with love, compassion, and tenderness.

The fourth evidence comes from Hosea 6:6, where the Lord says, "For I desire steadfast love and not sacrifice, the knowledge of God rather than burnt offerings." We also notice that the Lord wants His believers to have feelings of mercy because He is also merciful.

Finally, I cite the last verse in the book of Isaiah, where the Lord says, "Can a mother forget the baby at her breast and have no compassion on the child she has borne? Though she may forget, I will not forget you."

Here, God shows us the extent of His great and deep love, which surpasses a mother's love for her baby. There are many verses in the Holy Scriptures that show God's love and mercy.

Before concluding this topic, I'd like to clarify something I mentioned earlier: The human spirit is characterized by two hypostases, not three, even though there is also a spirit that gives life-like God. The main reason for this is that the human spirit cannot give anyone life, so we cannot elevate it to the rank of Trinity with three hypostases like God because only God can give life. And here I like to remind you that, while humans resemble God, we cannot elevate them to God's level of knowledge and ability because God is perfect in knowledge and ability while we are imperfect, and He is unlimited while we are limited.

I conclude the explanation with a beautiful phrase from the famous Sufi, Ibn al-Qayyim, in which he summarizes what I have written: "As for the correct opinion, the mind is its origin, and its principle is in the inner consciousness, its cultivation and fruit are in the head."

Exposition of the Theory of Fallen Angels

We begin with the first piece of evidence: We can contemplate the original sin mentioned by Saint Paul in his letter to Romans 5:12, in which he says, "Therefore, just as sin entered the world through one man, and death through sin, and in this way, death came to all people because all sinned." And in 1 Corinthians 15:22, he says, "For as in Adam all die, so in Christ all will be made alive." And I will cite here the last verse that came in John 3:16, "For God so loved the world that He gave His one and only Son, that whoever believes in Him shall not perish but have eternal life." I am not focusing here on the salvation of humanity from original sin, which has already occurred. I cited these verses to prove the reality of original sin, which Adam committed as stated in the Holy Scriptures, and his descendants were crushed by its weight until Christ came.

A Question Arises Here:

If Adam committed this sin, why should his children pay for it? And if we put Adam in a court of human judges, no matter what crime or sin he committed, the judges would not punish his children for whatever he did in terms of crime and sin unless they did the same thing as Adam.

I want to clarify and explain to you here that the sin

committed by Adam is the same sin that his descendants committed before they were born on this earth. Otherwise, God would not be just in punishing Adam's descendants. Since God has judged everyone to receive the same punishment, this means that Adam and his descendants were under the burden of sin due to a rebellion or disobedience they committed in the past. This is what I deduced from this judgment.

Note: There may be other facts about humans that God has not revealed to us, so we should always leave room for other possibilities because, as humans, we think, analyze, and draw conclusions based on limited knowledge and experience standards, and we cannot be certain about this matter as long as it remains a theory and God has not declared it.

The second piece of evidence is that we all believe that God created us out of love and that He wants everyone to be saved, as mentioned by the Apostle Paul in his first letter to Timothy 2:4, where he describes God: "Who desires all people to be saved and to come to the knowledge of the truth."

I propose a question here: If we assume that a skilled merchant entered a large deal, would he profit or lose? Of course, he should profit, even if it's a small percentage, because skilled and strong traders don't risk their money. So, how about God? When he enters a deal, does he profit or lose? Of course, he will profit at very high percentages. We notice here that when God created humans, He bet on winning a larger number of them. But as we see, many are led down the path of Satan and destruction, not to God. Does God lose this bet and lose all these spirits He created? Of course not. Jesus said in Matthew 22:14, "For many are called, but few are chosen." In this case, my theory is valid, which explains that God bargained with Satan on the fallen angels, and when He gave them a chance through the earthly body, He won the elite among them. As for those who did not follow the path of goodness and truth, they returned to where they came from, that is, to the abyss.

The third evidence is this: I mentioned it in the story *The Parable of the Prodigal Son*, as it is told in Luke 15:11–32. Here, we can compare the situation of the prodigal son to that of the sinful human who wants, of his own free will, to distance himself from his father, who symbolizes the heavenly Father, but the son repents, and his father accepts him. Suppose some angels disobeyed God and fell, then repented. Don't you think God can rehabilitate them so that they can return to Him? Just as He forgave and gave a second chance to Adam's children? It is written in Luke 15:7, "There will be more joy in heaven over one sinner who repents."

Among the parables that also illustrate this situation, we mention the parable of the lost sheep, which is mentioned in Matthew 18:12–14, where Jesus says: "What do you think? If a man owns a hundred sheep, and one of them wanders away, will he not leave the ninety-nine on the hills and go to look for the one that wandered off? And if he finds it, truly I tell you, he is happier about that one sheep than about the ninety-nine which didn't wander off. In the same way, your Father in heaven does not want any of these little ones to perish." This is a very important point that I want to draw your attention to, which is how God thinks and how He does not leave anyone righteous in good to perish, regardless of whether they are human or spirit. As stated in the Bible, "He will not leave him."

The fourth evidence that also illustrates this point is the parable of the Potter in Jeremiah 18:1–4, in which he says, "The word that came to Jeremiah from the Lord: 'Arise and go down to the potter's house, and there I will let you hear my words.' So,

I went down to the potter's house, and there he was working at his wheel. And the vessel he was making of clay was spoiled in the potter's hand, and he reworked it into another vessel, as it seemed good to the potter to do." If you continue reading the chapter, this was a warning from the Lord to the Jewish people who had strayed from the right path. But I cited this parable, through which I see that the Lord is able to rehabilitate good-natured humans even if they have gone astray. Here, I see that this parable applies to repentant souls and that God is able to provide a path to salvation for them. And one of the most important things is the redemption of Christ on the cross and his rehabilitation for the kingdom.

The fifth evidence is in the letter of the Apostle Paul to Ephesians 1:3–4, where he says: "Blessed be the God and Father of our Lord Jesus Christ, who has blessed us with every spiritual blessing in the heavenly places in Christ, just as He chose us in Him before the foundation of the world, that we would be holy and blameless before Him." Through the words of the Apostle, I observe that the souls of the chosen ones existed before the creation of the world, and if they did not, he would not have been able to declare it. Some theologians believe that these chosen spirits were in the mind of God before the creation of the world, but I find that illogical. The point I want to draw your attention to is that the spirits of humans existed before the creation of the world, and that is what I understood from the verse I mentioned now.

The sixth evidence is found in the Gospel of Matthew 11:10, where the prophecy says, "This is the one about whom it is written: 'I will send my messenger ahead of you, who will prepare your way before you.'" We also see here that God sent a chosen spirit to prepare the way for Jesus Christ. It is not unlikely here that this spirit is actually an angel as it came in the prophecy. What is the way to prevent the repentant fallen angels from coming in the same way and getting the opportunity to be saved? But we, as humans, cannot be certain and judge because perhaps there are other facts related to the nature of angels that we do not know.

The seventh evidence is Satan's temptation of Christ in the wilderness, which is mentioned in the three Gospels. I will choose one of them, which is Matthew 4:8–9, where it says: "Again, the devil took Him to a very high mountain and showed Him all the kingdoms of the world and their splendor. 'All this I will give You,' he said, 'if you will bow down and worship me.'" Here, we note that all the kingdoms on earth except for the kingdom of the Jews were subject to Satan, and he openly declared it, and Christ did not deny it. This raises the question: Why did God give all these kingdoms to Satan? Were they all wrong? However, this answer is not correct and accurate because many times, the Jews also sinned and worshiped gods other than their own, and yet the Lord did not abandon them. But why did God give up all these kingdoms and give them to Satan, as mentioned in the Gospels? There is only one answer: The inhabitants and kings of these kingdoms were subject to and loyal to Satan not only in this life but also before it.

The eighth evidence is Genesis 3:1–19: "Now the serpent was craftier than any of the wild animals the Lord God had made. He said to the woman, 'Did God really say, "You must not eat from any tree in the garden"?' The woman said to the serpent, 'We may eat fruit from the trees in the garden, but God did say, "You must not eat fruit from the tree that is in the middle of the garden, and you must not touch it, or you will die."'' 'You will not certainly die,' the serpent said to the woman. 'For God knows that when you eat from it, your eyes will be opened, and you will be like God, knowing good and evil.' When the woman saw that the fruit of the tree was good for food pleasing to the eye and also desirable for gaining wisdom, she took some and ate it. She also gave some to her man, who was with her, and he ate it.

"Then the eyes of both of them were opened, and they realized they were naked. Then the man and his woman heard the sound of the Lord God as he was walking in the garden in the cool of the day, and they hid from the Lord God among the trees of the garden. But the Lord God called to the man, 'Where are you?' He answered, 'I heard you in the garden, and I was afraid because I was naked, so I hid.' And He said, 'Who told you that you were naked? Have you eaten from the tree that I commanded you not to eat from?' The man said, 'The woman you put here with me—she gave me some fruit from the tree, and I ate it.' Then the Lord God said to the woman, 'What is this you have done?' The woman said, 'The serpent deceived me, and I ate.'

"So, the Lord God said to the serpent, 'Because you have done this, cursed are you above all livestock and all wild animals! You will crawl on your belly, and you will eat dust all the days of your life. And I will put enmity between you and the woman and between your offspring and hers; he will crush your head, and you will strike his heel.'

"To the woman, He said, 'I will make your pains in childbearing very severe; with painful labor, you will give birth to children. Your desire will be for your man, and he will rule over you.'

"To Adam, he said, 'Because you listened to your woman and ate fruit from the tree about which I commanded you, "You must not eat from it," cursed is the ground because of you; through painful toil, you will eat food from it all the days of your life. It will produce thorns and thistles for you, and you will eat the plants of the field. By the sweat of your brow, you will eat your food until you return to the ground since from it you were taken; for dust you are and to dust you will return.'"

I see the story of Adam and Eve's fall in this painting as symbolic and indicative of disobedience, but not as how some believe that Adam and Eve sinned by eating the fruit. And I'll try to prove it.

Firstly, if the tree of the knowledge of good and evil was a stumbling block for Adam and Eve, the Lord could have moved it or placed an angel to guard it.

Secondly, some believe that the sin of Adam and Eve revolves around the sexual act that God forbade them from engaging in, and this is also wrong because if God forbade them from doing such an act, then why did He create a penis for Adam and a vagina for Eve? He could have created them without a penis and a vagina. This belief is not logical.

What I find logical and realistic is that Adam and Eve desired to become like gods, instigated by Satan. Once they accepted the idea, it was counted as an unforgivable sin for them, and this is indeed what is mentioned in the book of Genesis, as we have seen in the text, and this is not an assumption. I see here that the sin is the same one committed by the fallen angels and by Adam and Eve.

A question arises: If God gave humans a chance to repent of sin through the redemption of the divine Savior, why don't angels also get the same chance if some of them regret their actions?

All that I have written about the nature of God and matters related to angels and humans is an attempt to understand God's purposes in creating humans on this earth and to comprehend the mystery of our existence and our role on this planet.

I believe that what I have presented in this book and this explanation of theological thoughts and intellectual deductions will be of great benefit to those who come after me and present new theological ideas and thoughts that bring them closer to the truth.

As Thomas Edison said after numerous experiments that did not lead to the discovery of electricity: "I have not failed. I've just found ten thousand ways that won't work." Meaning that these attempts led to the discovery of electricity. We are in an age where the tragedies of believers have escalated, and their questions have multiplied. It is the duty of the church to find the answers because the Lord has also raised it for this task.

Conclusion

At the end of this book, I would like to thank all those who helped me and stood with me in this spiritual work, which I consider to be my mission in this life.